SAVING THE FALLEN

VIOLA TEMPEST

CONTENTS

saving the fallen

VIOLA TEMPEST

CHAPTER 1

My steps echoed between the buildings. The streets looked empty, but I knew better. I knew she was here somewhere. And if she was here, so were they. I pulled my hood up to protect myself from the rain, but it barely helped. I was soaked through already, each step making a splash against the asphalt.

I turned onto a sidestreet, quickening my pace. There was this nagging feeling that someone—*something*—had their eyes on me. They probably did. It was too late to turn back now, and the girl was waiting

This neighborhood could be rough, even with the curfew in place. I didn't want to leave her alone for too long.

Darkness flooded the street; the streetlights barely seemed to work out here. I often kept away from this part of the city, but I had no choice tonight. Not if I wanted to help her. My blade was safely fastened to my side, hidden beneath my jacket, but I felt for it anyway. Making sure it was still there in case I should need it.

I rarely moved in this part of the city anymore. I had grown up here, ran around these same streets as a young child, but I hadn't been back in years. I barely recognized the streets anymore, the neighborhood in far worse shape than I remembered. Then again, that was the case for most neighborhoods in the underbelly of the city. Some shops were still in business, but most places had barred windows and graffiti all over the walls. I wondered what my grandfather would think of this place if he were still alive. I wondered what he would think of *me*.

The call had gone through less than an hour ago. A terribly frightened voice, begging for help. I left the house at once. These things were nothing if not time-sensitive. Once the angels had their sights set on someone, they tended to kill them quickly.

When the street ended, the only light source was a pink neon sign in one of the shop windows. I had to stop. Looking around, I searched for her. I didn't know what she looked like, but I knew her kind. I knew the fear in their eyes when they were desperate enough to come to me for help. I had seen it many times before.

"It's alright," I said, keeping my voice low. "I'm here."

I saw movement by one of the shop doors, and it creaked open. There she was. There was no mistaking those blue eyes. This was her, the Nephila. I reached a hand out for her.

"Come. We better get this over with."

"They will come." Her voice was shaking, and her hair was plastered to her pale face. She must have been caught in the rain as well. "I saw them in the sky."

"Yes," I said. "So, we must move quickly. Come."

She walked out onto the street. A bit taller than myself, but thin and brittle. I had never seen someone of her kind be so fragile. The fact that she even had powers surprised me. She didn't look strong enough to carry them. Well, she wasn't going to have to carry them for much longer.

"Give me your hand," I ordered. Her skin was cold to the touch, and I placed it over her heart with my hand on top. Her eye flitted around, anxiety written clearly across her face.

"Will this hurt?" she asked.

"Of course it will," I replied and rolled my eyes. Stripping a Nephila of their powers was no easy feat. "You know how this works, don't you?"

"Bits and pieces," she said, and I could see tears prickle in the corners of her eyes. I hoped she was strong enough to handle what was about to happen.

"I will remove your powers," I told her. "It's not a pleasant thing, but it will give you a chance at a normal life. It will keep *them* off your back. The angels do not interfere with humans as you well know."

"I will be human," she repeated, relief flooding her voice. I nodded.

"Yes, you will be human. Do you want me to proceed?"

She nodded, her jaw tense, and I could see her shaking. From fear or from cold, or maybe both. I closed my eyes. Taking a Nephila's powers was not a simple thing, but I managed to speed up the process over the years.

I called on my magic, let it flow through my body and into hers. When the electric static of the magic hit her, the Nephila gasped. I kept my hold on her hand strong; she couldn't move if this was going to work. Speaking the ancient words, I got started. I had to hold onto her arm to keep her steady once the spell took hold, but after a few moments, it seemed like she had gotten used to the feeling.

I severed the ties between her and the powers. It was delicate work, like a surgeon with his patient, but with so much more at stake. I could hear her crying, but it was too late to stop. I *wouldn't* stop. Not if it meant that she could be free.

"I can't...," she cried, the words coming out short and labored. "I can't go on."

"You can."

"It hurts." A sob escaped her. "It feels wrong..."

"Well, I'm sorry. But I can't stop now." My grip on her tightened, in case she tried to tear free. I didn't need much more time; I only had to pluck the last bits of the powers from her. They weren't strong, not like the others of her kind that I had encountered in the past. But they were strong enough to put her on *their* radar.

She was full on sobbing at this point. Her heart was beating slowly in her chest; I could barely feel it. Would she be able to handle it? There wasn't much of her powers left. I could feel it flow from her and into me, the strange force molding and wrapping around my own magic. This part wasn't pleasant for either of us; having another's powers mixed in with my own was a strange thing. They wouldn't be there for long, but they were enough to make the hairs stand on the back of my neck. The angelic powers of Nephilims were strange; they didn't feel right.

"Almost done," I assured her, hoping she would stay on her feet for the last few moments.

I found the last place where the powers needed to be severed and pushed my magic there. One last incision, and then she would be free. When the final tether snapped, the girl cried out, slumping against me.

"You need to be quiet," I hissed, a bit harsher than I had intended. "It's done. I have taken it all."

"Thank you," she sobbed, her face pressed against my chest, hands clutching my jacket. "Thank you."

"We need to move. Do you have a safe space to hide out for a few days?" I was eager to get back home, to get her powers out of my system, but I wanted to make sure she was safe. Or else this would all have been for nothing.

"I have a friend who can take me in," she said, her voice a little steadier than before. "She lives just outside the city."

"Good." I dug through my pockets, pulling out a small stack of credits. "Take these, get a ticket for one of the trains, and get to your friend. The sooner the better."

She took the credits, clutching them to her chest. "I don't know how to thank you."

"There is no need," I answered. "But we can't stay out here any longer. Get moving."

I followed her down the street, rounding the corner to get to the railroad office. It wasn't far, and hopefully, there would be space on one of the night routes out of the city.

I really wanted to get back home; her powers itched and twisted inside my body. But I couldn't just leave her out in the open like this. Not when they were around... somewhere. They usually were when a Nephila had been spotted by their scouts. And this girl wouldn't have come to me if she weren't on their radar.

Our steps echoed on the empty street, the rain just intensifying. I could hear the girl's teeth clattering, but I resisted the urge to give her my jacket. It was soaked; it wouldn't really do anything for her, and I needed it for myself. She would be fine once we got to the office.

"I feel strange," she whispered as we turned left.

"You will for a while," I told her. "It is to be expected. Your whole being has been altered, after all."

A Nephila choosing to get rid of their powers was getting more and more common. Finding a witch that was willing to help them get rid of them was another story altogether. The sisters in my coven weren't exactly thrilled that I extended my help to the Nephilim; they said it put an unnecessary target on my back. They were right about that, but I didn't care. The angels were powerful, but they couldn't stop me. They'd have to kill me first before I stopped helping those that needed it.

Even so, my sisters begged for me to stop. I understood their concern, but as their leader, they couldn't exactly stop me from doing it. I didn't want to fight with my sisters, but I couldn't watch an entire race get slaughtered just because of the crime of being born. It just wasn't right.

"There," I said and gestured to a big, white building ahead. "Will you be alright for the final bit? I need to get home."

The girl nodded. "I'll be fine. Thank you again. You cannot begin to understand what you have done for me."

I smiled. "Take care of yourself, alright?"

"You, too," she said and put a hand on my arm. "This world wouldn't be such a horrible place if there were more people like you in it."

She turned, looking over her shoulder at me one last time. I could feel the blood drain from my face as she started walking, only to stop in her tracks. I looked skyward, already knowing what I would see up there.

Angels. Descending from the sky and landing with graceful movements. I counted five. No, six. One by one, they blocked the street, their massive wings like a wall behind their strong bodies. I recognized the one in front. Gabriel.

A flicker of recognition flashed across his face; I had obviously made an impact the last time we met. I hoped the cut I made on his arm had left a scar. I had managed to stay in the shadows for a long time while helping the Nephilim. But for the past few months, Gabriel and his brothers seemed to know how to sniff me out.

The last time had been a close call, I must admit. I still had some pain in my left arm from that fight. But at least I got a hit on Gabriel himself, too. I remembered the surprised look on his face when my blade slashed across his arm. Not deep enough to actually hurt him badly, but the fact that I got a hit at all told him not to underestimate me. I straightened, pushing the girl behind me. Gabriel had a cold smile on his lips, and he narrowed his eyes as he regarded me.

"You just keep putting your nose where it doesn't belong, witch," he called out, his voice booming between the tall buildings. "This girl is ours. I suggest you walk away."

"Actually, she isn't yours," I called back, and I felt the girl clutching my arm from behind. She was crying, trying her best not to make a sound. She wasn't being very successful, however. I clutched my blade tighter and glared at him. "Not anymore."

I could hear him laugh, those eerily blue eyes almost glowing in the dark. "You think that just because you took her powers, she is no longer an abomination? The angel that sired her is still her father. Power or not, she *is* a Nephila."

I felt the girl shaking behind me, and I cast a quick glance over my shoulder at her. Her blue eyes were wide and her jaw slack. Despite her father, I doubted she had ever actually met an angel before. Most Nephilim grew up in human cities, and she was most likely not an exception. They must seem absolutely terrifying to her! Despite the angels' beauty, there was also a brutality there that couldn't be ignored. I reached for my blade.

"She is human now," I called out. "You have no business interfering with the humans."

Gabriel smirked. "Agree to disagree." His eyes were trained on the girl. "Let's end this nonsense now."

Blade in one hand and my magic at the ready, I still felt a chill run through me when two of them rose high up in the air, the other three coming down toward us. I'd never gotten used to this part. The fighting. The killing. But what choice did I have? It was either them or us.

"Stay behind me," I said to the girl, almost wishing I hadn't been so hasty to take away her powers.

It wouldn't have been much, but it would've been a small help if she could fight, too. At least, she would've been able to do *something* to defend herself. Now, she was entirely dependent on me. I couldn't even use the angelic powers I had taken from her for an even match; they were a distraction in my limbs more than anything else. It was as if my own magic recognized them as something foreign, something to be worked around.

I was just going to have to try and ignore its presence in my body. I called upon a shielding spell, and I pushed it around us for protection. It wouldn't hold for long, but it would at least stop the angels for a few minutes. The air flickered as the shield wrapped around our bodies, and I saw irritation in Gabriel's face. He knew what I could do. Knew I wouldn't make this easy for them.

"As soon as you can," I said to her. "You run. Run like hell. Get to the office and get to your friend."

She didn't answer, but I hoped she would do as I said. I glanced skyward again; the two angels up there were like shadows in the sky. They would attack at the same time as the ones on the ground. Coming at us at different angles would make it difficult to hold the shield. But I couldn't worry about the shield; there was no use. I just had to worry about fighting back.

It happened all at once, just like I had anticipated. I crouched down and slammed my hand on the wet asphalt. I screamed out the incantation, making the ground shake and the air shoot out from where I was standing. The angels flinched and were forced to back up a step as the wind knocked against them. It was just a temporary solution, a way to knock them off their balance.

Without wasting another second, I charged. I slid my blade against Gabriel's porcelain skin, just barely grazing his arm with the steel. Blood dripped onto the street, but it was just a scratch. The angels in the sky dove toward the girl, and I rushed for her, just barely getting away from the angels on the ground. I shoved the blade up, burying it in the throat of one of them. The gurgled sound that escaped him before the life left his body was enough to make me shiver.

The other one was too far away, but I put my free hand out in front of my body and let my magic do the work. I felt my power grip him, like a chain that wrapped around his every limb, and I slammed him down onto the asphalt. The ground cracked as he landed, his cry echoing in the night. I hope I broke something.

I turned, just as Gabriel got his hands on me. His strong arms wrapped around me, pinning my arms against my sides. *Damn it.* I could feel his power radiate through his hands, making my skin burn where he touched me. I gritted my teeth, flipping my blade in my hand so I could drive it into his thigh.

Gabriel roared into my ear, and his grasp on me loosened enough so that I could get away. The girl was screaming, surrounded by three of them. I rushed toward them, but I was pulled back, a massive hand grabbing my hair. I placed my hand over his, shooting heat onto his skin. It wasn't until I could practically smell flesh burning that he released his grip on me, and I whirled around, slashing at him with my blade.

Gabriel backed off, evading the steel time and time again. I heard the girl scream again; the other angels had her cornered. I spoke the words for another spell, aiming my magic at them, but Gabriel grabbed my arm, jerking it to the side before I could do anything. I yelled out in pain, turning to him to avoid him breaking my arm. The anger was clear on his face; he was obviously done with me at that point.

"You're not getting her," I hissed, trying to ignore the pain that shot through my arm.

"Oh, but we are," he teased, glancing over at his brothers. "She'll be dead before you can take another step."

I was losing control of the situation. There were just too many of them, and I couldn't keep them all away from her. Didn't mean I wouldn't try, though.

Before Gabriel got a chance to react, I drove my blade into his abdomen, and as he screamed, I sprinted for the other three. Without my weapon, I had to rely on my other strength. I lunged for the one closest to me, jumping onto his back, and grabbed his wings. I gathered all the fire in my body, making the feathers smoke as the heat spread through them. He screamed and tried to get me off, flouncing around in his panicked state, but I didn't let go.

One strong arm then reached for me, dragging me by the leg to the ground. I flinched when I landed on the hard street, but there was no time to stop. I managed to grab hold of the girl's dress, and I pulled her until she was behind me. Tears were streaming down her face, and her skin was ice cold to the touch. I hoped she wasn't going into shock. She needed to run, needed to get out.

"End this now."

Gabriel's voice was heard behind the others. So, I didn't manage to hurt him badly enough then. Hopefully, my blade pierced something vital in there, at least. I conjured another shield around us, keeping them out for another short while. It wouldn't be enough. I had already used so much of my powers when I helped the girl, and I risked burning out. My protection spell wouldn't be strong enough, not when I had already depleted so much of my magic.

They would tear through the barrier in no time, and I wouldn't be able to take them on all at once. I could feel their angelic powers trying to break through the shield, and I kept speaking the words to keep it in place. My hands were shaking with the effort, but I couldn't stop. I wouldn't win this fight. Not on my own. So, we had to run. And we had to run fast.

"Get ready," I said to the girl. My hands were shaking so much that it felt like they might fall off. I wouldn't be able to hold for much longer. Gabriel was coming closer; he was right outside the barrier, flanked by his brothers.

"Enough!" he yelled, his voice cold.

Suddenly, something moved behind the angels. I just barely saw a figure between the gaps of their massive forms. If a human came into this mess, they would die.

Stay away, I silently begged, hoping they would be smart enough to get back inside. I wasn't going to be able to protect a human as well as the girl and myself.

Then one of the angels gasped, right before a blade sliced across his throat.

My blade.

CHAPTER 2

For a moment, time seemed to stand still. The dead angel fell to the ground, seemingly in slow motion as his brothers turned, their focus completely off me and the girl. Then chaos erupted.

I heard the clang of my blade hit the street, and I dove for it. The cold steel felt reassuring in my hand. I charged at the angel closest to me, driving my weapon into his back, right between his wings. His scream echoed in the air. But I didn't stop to see him fall, just pulled my weapon out and turned to the next. Just to find out that someone else had gotten there first.

A man, just as tall and broad as the angels, held a sword in his hand. He moved quickly, the rain making his dark hair fall over his eyes. That didn't seem to slow him down, though. He dodged the angel's attempts to strike him as if he could anticipate what was going to happen next. The grace and strength with which he moved told me that he had done this before. He was obviously trained, but I couldn't understand how. Maybe he was also a Nephila. Or maybe he was just human, sick of the angels taking over more and more of this city. When he drove his sword through the angel, our eyes met.

"Move."

His deep voice shot through me, waking me from my temporary trance. I whirled around, realizing that Gabriel hadn't attempted to get to me. I soon understood why. The angel towered over the girl, and he stood close enough to touch her. She backed away, and both I and the stranger charged for them.

I cast a flame through my fingers, releasing it in an attempt to knock Gabriel off his feet. He didn't even flinch when the spell hit him. He must've put up a shielding spell of his own, or whatever the angelic equivalent was. And I was wiped; there wasn't very much left in me.

The stranger was in front of me, his long legs giving him an advantage in speed. I watched as Gabriel reached for the girl, and I quickened my pace. My magic wouldn't help; only steel could end this. The man seemed to think so, too, because he swung back his sword, only to aim it right at Gabriel's heart.

But he was too late.

Gabriel's arms were wrapped around the girl, a strange gentleness to the embrace. I heard her neck snap in the next moment, and my heart stopped.

She flailed to the ground, and just as the stranger's sword was about to hit its target, Gabriel took flight. I flung my blade to the ground, screaming out an incantation to the sky. It didn't work—Gabriel was already too far gone.

I swore under my breath, then rushed to the girl's side. Her eyes were staring blankly ahead, her body limp and lifeless. Even though I knew it was pointless, I tried to feel for a pulse. Nothing. Of course not. I swore again, getting onto my feet.

The man stood a few feet away, breathing heavily after everything that had gone down. He was looking at me as if trying to assess what kind of person I was. Whether I needed to perish also, same as the angels, or if I could be trusted. I picked my blade up and wiped the blood off on my shorts. They were ruined anyway.

"Who are you?" I asked. There was something off about him, something that didn't seem quite right. I just couldn't put my finger on it.

He straightened himself, his breathing calmer than a moment ago. He sheathed his sword, then he turned his eyes back onto me.

"My name is Castiel."

Castiel? I frowned. That name was angelic.

Whoever his mother had been, she had some nerve to give her son such a name, even if he were a Nephila. I didn't think he was, though. I swallowed, glancing down at the girl. So close. She had been so close to freedom. "I need to bury her," I whispered, more to myself than to him.

He answered anyway. "No. You need to come with me."

I looked up at him, brows knitted together. "Come with you? Why the hell would I do that?"

Castiel was standing right in front of me, and I could feel the warmth radiating from his skin. Then he glanced up at the sky. "You don't want to be here when they return for their corpse. In fact, I doubt you even want to be in this city when they do."

I took a step back. "I can handle myself, thank you very much."

A small smile tugged at his lips. "I know. You *are* Danika Ryker, leader of the local coven."

I stared at him. "You know me?"

"I know *of* you. Most of my kind do."

Who the hell was this guy? And what did he mean, *his kind?* "They won't return for a while. I need to bury her."

He grabbed my hand, and before I could pull free, he nodded to the sky. "Look up."

Fuck. The fluttering of wings was all I could see at first. Then they came closer. I shook my head. "No. I won't just leave her here. We'll fight!"

"The girl is dead," Castiel practically shouted, an

edge to his voice. "There is nothing you can do for her anymore. They outnumber us, and they *will* kill us if we stay." His grip on my hand tightened. "So, we *run*."

My entire body screamed for me to stay, but I knew he was right. There were at least eight angels in the sky, and they would be here in no time. So, I nodded, and we took off down the street. He seemed to know where to go, and his firm hold of my hand forced me to follow.

"My coven!" I shouted. "We can go there! The angels won't get through the wards."

"That's the first place they'll look!" Castiel shouted back. "I have a place we can hide."

"If you think I'm leaving my sisters unprotected, then you're an idiot." I tried to pull free, but he was much stronger than me. I whispered a spell, burning his hand until he let go. We then came to a halt, and a chill ran through me as he stared me down.

"Are you truly so foolish?" he growled. "They will find us if we don't move." He tried to grab my hand again, but I jumped back.

"If they go to my coven as you said, then my sisters are in danger."

"I thought you said the wards would hold."

They would. They *probably* would. But I couldn't just go with him without knowing my coven would be safe. "I'm going there, with or without you."

He stepped closer, his face inches from mine. "*No.*"

I squared my jaw. "And how do you suppose you'll

stop me? I'm a witch. I can knock you out cold right here on the street while barely lifting a finger."

"And *I* can simply fling you over my shoulder and carry you away," he said. "I could knock you out cold too, if you prefer. Besides, your magic needs replenishing. You still need to get rid of the Nephila's powers. So, what will it be? Will you walk on your own accord, or do I have to carry you?"

"I'd like to see you try," I tested him, voice low and dripping with rage.

"Very well."

I couldn't hold back my squeal when he lifted me from the ground and slung me over his shoulder. One hand was firmly placed on the back of my thighs, and then he simply started walking.

"What the *fuck* do you think you're doing?"

"Getting us out of a bad situation," he answered. "If you have a problem with that, then you're dumber than you look."

I grabbed onto his shoulders, heaving myself up so I could look at him. Castiel raised his face, looking up at me. He needed to shift his grip to hold onto my legs, and then slowly let me sink down the front of his body. But he didn't let me go entirely. Simply lowered me enough so that we were face-to-face.

"You have exactly two seconds to let me go," I snarled. "Or I'll burn you again."

"Oh, please do," he teased with a grin. "I don't mind some pain."

Asshole. "You can't make me leave my coven!" I screamed at him, trying to calm my racing heart.

"I can, and I will," he simply responded and started walking again. "The angels are looking for you, and I kinda need you to stay alive."

"Why? I'm no one to you."

"True," he said. "But I think you can help me with a problem."

"Okay, this is ridiculous," I snapped. "Let me down. *Now.*"

"Don't you want to know about my problem?"

"I'm sure you have plenty of problems you need to talk about, but no, I can't say that I do." I placed one hand at the base of his neck, calling upon enough heat to sting him. "Now let me down."

Castiel sighed, but at least he did as I said. "We need to keep moving," he said. "Come with me, and I can take you to your coven once things settle down."

"I am perfectly capable of getting there myself," I told him. Then I heard a noise somewhere behind us. We both turned to look, and I saw Castiel's entire body tense.

"They're close."

I couldn't see them, but I knew he was right. I could hear their wings somewhere in the distance, could hear their voices as someone shouted a command. We didn't have time to argue.

"Fine," I gave in, "I'll come to your safe spot. But only until they leave."

It looked like he wanted to argue some more, but then he seemed to think better of it. "Come on then."

He led the way through the winding streets of the city. Neon lights and concrete structures blended with the trash and odd bits of greenery here and there. I was thankful for the curfew keeping the humans indoors, but I was certain some of them were looking out their windows at the angels roaming their streets. No doubt some had seen the fight earlier, too. I hoped someone would take care of the girl's body tomorrow. The thought of her lying there—cold and wet and just *gone* —was unbearable.

Castiel rushed me down to the docks, the rain making the water ripple and break among the vessels there. I kept looking over my shoulder, expecting Gabriel or one of his brothers to appear. They didn't, but I had no doubt in my mind that they were still looking for us. They went down some stairs until they reached a simple, wooden door in one of the small buildings surrounding the water. It didn't look like much, definitely not strong enough to keep any angels out.

"This is your safe place?" I asked. "A wooden door and a dock worker's hut?"

"Just get inside," he huffed, holding the door open for me.

I felt a ripple cut through me as I stepped over the doorstep. There was magic in here. Something to protect the place from unwanted visitors. I gasped, staring at him. "You had it warded? How?"

"You and your sisters aren't the only witches in this city," Castiel said and locked the door behind him. "I know people."

So, he had another witch protect the space. That made me feel slightly better, I had to admit. The likelihood of the angels searching for us in such a place was slim, anyway. The wards just made things a bit more secure.

"How long do you think we'll have to stay here?" I asked and looked around. The small space was modestly decorated, with only a large bed, some chairs, and a table. Some books were scattered across the floor beside the bed, and I frowned. Paper books? I hadn't seen any of those in years. My grandfather had some when he was still alive, but they were falling apart by the end. Seemed impractical.

"Best to stay through the night," Castiel mumbled. "They tend to stay away during the day, so we should be safe by morning."

Even though I knew he was right, it irked me that I had to stay until morning. So much could happen during those hours, and I couldn't stop thinking about the risk of the angels coming into the coven in search of me. My sisters could hold their own, and the wards, hopefully, did their part, but the angels were strong. Their powers were so different from ours; it was sometimes hard to fend off.

"You don't have to just stand there," Castiel huffed again and slumped down onto one of the chairs. "Sit."

I placed myself opposite him, the table separating us. "How did you find us?" I asked. "Earlier."

"I was looking for you," he coyly muttered as if that wasn't strange at all. "When I saw that they were coming, I decided to step in."

He had been looking for me? "Why were you looking for me?"

"I told you. I have a problem that you can help me with."

"I don't offer magic solutions to humans," I said. "None of us do; it's the law."

Castiel smirked. "I'm well aware of the law."

"And you just don't care about it."

"It doesn't apply to me," he said, leaning back against his chair.

I scoffed. "Are you always this arrogant?"

He shrugged. "It's not arrogant if it's true."

"Yeah, no." I shook my head. "Definitely arrogant."

He leaned closer, placing his arms on the table. His blue eyes bore into mine, and there was a hint of amusement on his face. "It doesn't apply to me because I'm not human."

I laughed. So, this was one of those fanatics who were convinced that they were something *more* than just a regular human. I'd met someone like this before. He was convinced he was a witch, too, despite not showing any signs of magical abilities.

"No?" I asked. "What are you then?"

"I'm an angel."

CHAPTER 3

I clutched the blade in my hand. "What do you mean you're an angel?"

Castiel threw his hands out to the side. "Exactly what I said. I'm an angel."

I tried to make out whether he was joking, or if he was simply mad. Castiel looked completely serious, though. "I'm not sure I'm following."

He smiled. "Surely, someone who deals with my kind as often as you do is aware of the fallen."

A fallen angel? I had heard of those, but I'd never actually seen one. Or maybe I had, and I just didn't know it. I looked him over. For an angel to fall, he must've done something truly bad. Or maybe just bad in the eyes of the angels. Their laws were ridiculous, evidenced by their hunt of the Nephilim.

"How do I know you're just not making it up?" I asked.

Castiel glanced down at himself as if his massive form was proof enough. And sure, he had the build of an angel. His eyes were almost the same eerie shade of blue that the angels tended to have, only not quite as striking.

"How did it happen?" I asked, deciding to humor him for a moment.

He shrugged his face, hardening for a moment. "I made the mistake of falling in love."

"With a human," I filled in. It was well known that it was completely forbidden for angels and humans to be together. After all, the Nephilim were being hunted and killed every day. A product of their parents' forbidden affection.

"Where is she now?" I asked, although I wasn't sure I wanted to know what the angels did to the humans who fell in love with their kind. I couldn't imagine it was something good.

"Six feet underground, I would imagine."

I noticed his clenched fists, his squared shoulders. "You don't know?"

He shook his head. "When we were caught, I was called back to Heaven. Held prisoner until a verdict had been set for my future. They took my powers. My wings. They took *her*."

My head was spinning. He looked so... sad. So beaten down. Maybe he wasn't making it up. Maybe he really was one of the fallen. "I'm sorry," I whispered quietly. "That's horrible."

"It was a long time ago." Castiel stood, huffing out a breath. "I would like to move forward. And that's where you come in."

"I don't know why I'm a part of any of this," I said.

Castiel smiled. "I need you to get me back into Heaven."

Had I heard him right? "You want me to do *what*?"

"I need you to restore my powers again," he said. "I want my wings back. I want to go home."

That settled it. He *was* insane. "I don't even know how to begin to do something like that!" I exclaimed, leaning my arms on the table, my blade still in a firm grip. "I help the Nephilim. I give them a chance to live by taking their powers. I protect them from your kind. Why would I give Heaven another angel to add to their forces? Your lot isn't exactly treating us well down here."

He was silent for a moment as if he hadn't even considered this. "Wouldn't it be advantageous to have an angel on your side?"

I couldn't hold back the humorless laugh that escaped me. "The only interactions I've ever had with pureblooded angels have been brutal. Senseless fights, and like you saw earlier, the slaughter of the innocent.

Forgive me if I don't believe you'll be on my side once you get what you need from me."

Castiel stood and placed himself right in front of me, and his eyes burned into mine. But he seemed a bit... Off. Like he wasn't really looking at me, but just focused his eyes on my face while deep in thought.

"I see you're going to need some convincing," he said after a few moments. I burst out laughing.

"You think? Are you honestly surprised that I didn't just bow down to you and agree at once? Am I the first witch you've ever met, or what?"

"No," he mumbled, brows furrowed. "I told you before, I know others of your kind."

"Yeah, yeah," I said, waving him off. "I just meant that you seem to be under the impression that my kind and yours are on good terms."

"You help the Nephilim."

"You are no Nephilim. They have done nothing wrong. The angels, however..."

"Okay." He raised his hands in a placating gesture. "I get it; we're no..."

"Angels?" I suggested, and one corner of my mouth curved up into a grin.

"Was that a joke?"

"Apparently not a very good one," I said and pushed up onto my feet. "Look, I'm not the person you're looking for. I can't help you."

"But..."

"No." I stopped smiling. "I'm not getting into any

angel business. Can you imagine what they might do to me, to my sisters, if they found out that I helped you? You violated their laws, as stupid as those laws might be, and you were given your sentence. I will not meddle with that."

Castiel had a certain look on his face. I couldn't quite pinpoint what that look meant. "Do you honestly think they won't come after you or your sisters regardless if you help me or not?"

"Maybe," I said. "And if they do, we'll defend ourselves."

A dry laugh escaped him. "Are you even aware of the power they possess? What they can do?" He shook his head. "I don't think you do. And you've pissed off one of the archangels. Gabriel will not stop until you're dead."

As if Gabriel wasn't already pissed off at me before tonight. Castiel didn't need to know that though. I took one step closer, inches away from his massive form. I raised my chin and looked him right in the eye. "If they're so bad, why do you want to go back to Heaven?"

His eyes flickered between my eyes and a spot behind me like he couldn't quite keep eye contact. "It is my home."

Bull. Shit. There was obviously more to the story, something else he wasn't telling me, but I didn't push. It didn't matter anyway; I wasn't doing it. "You need to find your own way back to Heaven. Sorry."

I started walking toward the door, but Castiel

rushed in front of me, blocking my path. "You can't just go out there," he said. "It's still dark."

"If you think you can stop me..."

"I can, and I will." He towered over me, no doubt trying to intimidate me with his size. It must be excruciating to not have his powers, to just have to rely on his physical traits. For a moment, I imagine what he must've been like before. With his wings. With the piercing blue eyes of the angels. He must've been quite a sight.

He was quite a sight *now*.

"Get out of my way," I hissed, voice low. Castiel shook his head.

"Wait until morning. They're still out there."

"They are *always* out there," I snapped, trying to push him out of my way. But he was solid as a rock. Fine. I'd just have to let my magic do the moving for me then.

With one hand placed on his chest, I pulled on a spell. Castiel didn't seem to understand what I was doing at first, and by the time he realized, it was too late. With a pull, I dragged him away from the door. I nailed him against the back wall of the small hut, and to my surprise, he almost tore free of the invisible binds that I'd put on him. But my magic held strong, and with one last look over my shoulder, I walked out.

The docks were quiet, but there would be workers there in just a short while. I hurried toward the city center. I needed to get back home, and even though I knew it was far too risky, I wanted to check on the Nephila.

There were people around, early risers who needed to get to work. I walked quickly, my hood pulled up. I couldn't wait to get out of my damp clothes, but that would have to wait. I approached the spot carefully, blade and magic ready.

When I got there, the spot had been cleared as if nothing had gone down there at all. The angels had no doubt taken their dead, maybe even the girl. I doubted they would've cleaned up the blood, but someone had. A neighbor who had witnessed the whole thing, maybe.

Mixed emotions battled in my chest. I was glad to not have to look at the dead bodies, but I wanted to know what happened to the girl's body. I bit my cheek. Such a waste. She only wanted to be free, had been so close to it. I didn't even know her name. I hoped someone would miss her. The friend she talked about perhaps. Surely, that friend would wonder what had happened when she didn't turn up. But I suspected that they wouldn't wonder for long. The Nephilim usually ended up in the hands of the angels. That was just the reality of the situation.

There was no use dwelling on it. I knew I would anyway, but I forced myself to leave the place and head back to the coven. It wasn't very far, despite my place being in a completely different part of the city.

I hopped onto a train, getting off after just ten minutes. Then I walked as fast as I could to the seemingly run-down house at the edge of a barren field. Just a mask, of course. An attempt to protect our anonymity, but it didn't work very well. Mostly everyone knew the witches lived there.

I crossed the property line, and the building changed into what it truly was. A modern, large house with every comfort we could possibly need. I was quite proud of its design. Tall windows and the latest technology to make life as comfortable as possible. It was quiet when I walked through the front doors. Usually, my sisters were up at this hour, most of us more comfortable at night.

I decided to cleanse myself of the Nephila's powers. It crawled around inside my limbs like smoke, and I itched to be rid of it. I closed my eyes and called on a spell to burn it out of my system. It wasn't a pleasant thing, but it was just something I had to endure. It would feel better afterwards.

Little by little I purged myself from the girl's powers. I felt lighter by the second until I couldn't feel a trace of it any longer. I sighed. I needed to eat something to get my energy back. I was close to burning out with all the magic I had used tonight.

The kitchen was empty, and I quickly fixed myself some food. There were leftovers from dinner that I just quickly heated up. I tried to listen for my sisters as I ate, but I didn't see or hear a soul.

And then I did.

Frowning, I swallowed the last of my food and then left the kitchen. I hurried up the stairs toward the sound of voices. Suddenly, I stopped in my tracks when one of my sisters, Tatia, came rushing toward me. Her dark eyes were glassy like she had been crying, and there was a gash on her right cheek. I placed my hand over it, feeling the raised flesh of the cut. Tatia pulled away.

"Where have you been?" she asked, an edge to her voice.

"Tatia, what's wrong?" I asked back, forcing her to look at me so I could see her injury. "Who did this to you?"

She shook her head. "Later. Come with me."

I followed her as she hurried back through the hall-way. "Tatia, please tell me what happened! You look like you've just seen a ghost."

"We were searching for you everywhere," she said, ignoring my question. "I had girls out there trying to find you. Where were you, Danika?"

"I had some things to take care of."

She side-eyed me. "If you were meeting up with one of the Nephilim again..."

"Enough." I grabbed her arm, forcing her to stop. "I help the Nephilim, and I will keep doing that. We've had this discussion before, Tatia. Now, tell me what's wrong."

She faced me, burying her dark eyes into mine. "There was an attack."

It felt like someone poured a bucket of freezing water over my head. "An attack?"

"The angels came. Seemed to think you were here,

which you should've been. When you weren't, and we wouldn't tell them anything, they—"

This was exactly what I had been afraid of. "Is someone hurt?" I interrupted, setting off toward the voices of my sisters again. Tatia was right on my heel. I reached one of the bedrooms, where a cluster of women had gathered. They were crying.

"What happened?" I whispered. A dozen eyes were suddenly on me. And then I saw the lifeless body of Yvette, one of our youngest. Lying on the floor, surrounded by her sisters, her dead eyes stared back at me.

CHAPTER 4

I felt my knees hit the carpeted floor before I realized that I had fallen. "Oh, God."

"God won't help you now," Tatia said and passed me through the door to the bedroom. "His angels were already here."

"How did they get in?" I asked in a weak voice. This was *exactly* what I had been afraid of. This was all my fault. If I had just gone home right away, I could've been here. I could've strengthened our wards; I could have fought them off!

"There were so many of them," Tatia explained

"Too many. We held off for as long as we could, but Yvette got in their way."

I rose to my feet, walking over to my sisters and the dead body. There was no hatred in their eyes when they looked at me, but I almost wished there were. I was their leader, and I had failed them. I had caused the death of a young girl because I angered the angels.

"They will pay for this," I hissed.

"What's the point?" one of my sisters said. "They'll just come back with more."

"They were looking for you, Danika. Do you realize the target you are putting on the coven's back with the way you meddle in their business?" Tatia placed a hand on my shoulder. "We don't blame you; we know your intentions are good. But this cannot happen again."

I nodded. She was right; it couldn't.

"We managed to throw them out, but they made it clear that they were coming back for you." Tatia shook her head. "I don't know how we're supposed to ward them off, to be honest."

I gnawed on my bottom lip, my eyes placed firmly on Yvette's body on the ground. I could stay and fight, and risk another one of my sisters getting hurt. Or I could leave. I could make sure the angels knew I was no longer with my coven, and then I'd just... Go. Hide. I don't know where I was supposed to go, but that was a problem for later.

"You will not suffer because I have angered the

angels," I said slowly. I could feel everyone's eyes on me as I spoke.

"I don't like that look on your face, Danika," Tatia answered, looking at me with a raised brow.

I shook my head. "There aren't really very many alternatives."

"What do you mean?"

"I'll leave," I told them. "I'll make sure the angels know that I'm no longer inside this house, and then I'll leave. They can't hunt me forever; it's just until the dust settles."

Tatia didn't look convinced. "They might think we know where you are."

"I'll make sure they don't."

"How?"

I chewed on my lip. "Not entirely sure. I'll figure it out."

She gave me another look but seemed at least willing to let the subject go. We both turned to the rest of our sisters, and I stared at the dead body on the floor. I swallowed a lump in my throat.

"We should bury her," I said to them all. "Lay her to rest."

Unfortunately, we had a place for our fallen sisters just south of our property. It didn't happen very often, but when it did, we wanted to bury our own close to home. It was only right.

We all helped out in digging Yvette's grave. It could've been done within minutes if we used our magic, but it was customary to bury our dead ourselves, without any help from our powers. My hands were red and blistered by the time we were done, and then we lowered her into her resting place. Each of my sisters covered Yvette with soil, and once we were done, it was almost evening again.

"A senseless death," I whispered, wiping the sweat from my forehead. "And I'll make sure something like this never happens again. Let us bow our heads and remember our sister. Let us remember Yvette."

A moment passed. Then another. The sounds of the city outside our home filtered in through the silence, the sound of trains mixed in with the bustle of the evening crowd. I wondered if they would come out again tonight. The angels. No doubt they would. And they would be looking for me.

I quickly cleaned up and threw some things inside a bag. I wanted to get out of the house before the sun went down entirely, and I needed to think. I needed a way to make it known that I was no longer inside this house. That my sisters had no clue as to where I was hiding. And I needed an actual place to hide in.

For some reason, Castiel's face popped into my head. He was most likely out there somewhere, waiting for me to leave the warded borders of my property. I couldn't imagine that he was particularly happy with the stunt I pulled earlier, but what choice did I have? I needed to get back home. And not even a day later, I had to leave again. Maybe he could be of use to me in my attempts to find a place to hide. Maybe I could even hole out in his hut for a day or two until I figured out what to do next.

I jumped when the door to my bedroom opened, the sudden sound startling me out of my thoughts. Tatia stood there, leaning against the doorframe. She looked so tired. Her lovely dark hair laid in a mess, scrunched up on top of her head. There were dark circles under her eyes, and I wondered when she had last eaten. The cut on her cheek still looked open and fresh.

"Come here," I said and reached for her. Tatia sat down on the edge of my bed, and I grabbed her chin to get a good look at her injury. "Have you even washed this?" I asked.

Tatia shook her head. "There wasn't any time."

I sighed and got up. "Well, we need to wash it now. Come with me."

I took her to my bathroom and watched as she rinsed the wound out with water. We returned to my bedroom once I was satisfied with its cleanliness, and I started to rummage through my salves. I wasn't the most proficient with the healing herbs that grew in our garden, but I knew enough to mix them together into potion. I handed her a small tube with a minty green mixture inside.

"Put this on it every night until it starts to close up."

Tatia nodded. "I will. Thank you."

No one said anything for several minutes. Tatia sat hunched over. Broken. She was the one who brought

Yvette to our coven. A younger sister of a friend, I believe.

"I'm so sorry this happened," I said before she got a chance to speak. "I really, really am."

"I know you are, Danika. And it's not your fault. Not really. If the angels weren't meddling in things outside of Heaven, this wouldn't have happened."

She was right about that. Things hadn't always been this way. My grandfather often told the story of when the angels first came down from Heaven. He told me about the way the humans had lived before then. I couldn't even imagine such a life. Without a nightly curfew, without having to look up at the sky as those massive men came toward you. How peaceful it must have been.

"I'll leave in just a moment," I said, slinging my bag across my body. Tatia straightened, and I thought I saw a flicker of fear in those deep, brown eyes. "It's alright," I said again and cupped her cheek. "It's not forever. I'll be back as soon as I know you are not in danger anymore. You can hold your own in the meantime."

She swallowed. "Make sure to stay safe, alright? Don't be an idiot."

"I'll try not to," I said, smiling at her. Tatia was a good friend. A good sister. "I'm leaving you in charge while I'm away, okay?"

"Me?" she asked, seeming surprised. "Wouldn't one of the older sisters be better?"

I shook my head. "No, I want it to be you. You're the best for the job, Tatia. I promise."

It almost looked like she was about to disagree, but then she nodded. "Thank you, Danika."

"Don't thank me yet," I said, trying to sound upbeat. "Heavy is the head that wears the crown."

Some of the tension eased from Tatia's face, and she rolled her eyes at me. "Right. Because being our leader is so burdensome for you."

I smirked. It really wasn't. I was the leader in name, but we did most things as a family—my Nephilim activities aside.

"Will you tell the others that I have gone?" I asked. "I don't want to disturb them anymore tonight."

She nodded. "Of course."

I ran into some more of my sisters on my way out, and we said our goodbyes. I hurried outside, eager to put some distance between myself and the coven when something caught my eye. No, not something. *Someone.*

"Well, well. Fancy meeting you here."

Castiel fell into step beside me as I walked down the street. "Still angry about before?" I asked, keeping my voice light. He scowled at me.

"*Still?* It was this morning."

"You really shouldn't hold a grudge, you know."

He huffed out a short laugh. "Right. Where are you heading? Are there more Nephilim that need to die tonight?"

I stopped dead in my tracks. "What did you say?"

Castiel raised his hands. "Sorry, sorry. That was low."

I couldn't believe he would even joke about that. I narrowed my eyes at him.

"One of my sisters just died. The angels attacked them all."

His face fell. "They came here?"

"As you said they would." I hoisted my bag higher on my shoulder. "And now I have to leave for a while. I just need to make sure the angels know that I'm no longer with my coven."

He nodded. "Well, it's after curfew. If I know them like I think I do, they'll come out and look for us both soon enough."

I frowned. "Look for us both? Why would they look for you?"

Castiel looked at me like I was stupid. "Did you miss the part where I killed a few of them last night? Not to mention, there's some... history there."

Of course. I hadn't even considered the fact that Gabriel and the rest probably weren't too fond of Castiel either after what had happened. "So, what's your plan?"

"I told you last night," he said. "I'm going back to Heaven."

"I mean, what's your plan right now? If the angels come for you?"

"Fight."

"There will be a lot more than last night," I warned him. "Fighting them would be a death sentence."

"Alright, no fighting then. I'll just follow you around until you help me." He smirked at me. "What is your plan? Wait until they show up, let them know that you're not living with the coven anymore, and then hope that they'll let you go on your merry way?"

"I haven't..." I fell silent, hating the smug look on his face.

"You don't know, do you? You don't have a plan."

"I'll figure it out," I snapped, wanting to wipe that look off his face. "I haven't exactly had time to think it all through."

"Fair enough," he said. "But we should probably get moving. You don't want them to find you right outside your coven, do you?"

Well, he was right about that. We walked in silence down the empty streets, and I could hear them before I saw them. Castiel glanced my way, his features schooled into neutrality, but I saw the tension there. He was nervous.

"Maybe get your sword out from its sheath," I hissed while grabbing my blade from its place inside my jacket. "Best to get ready."

He did as I said, and then we simply waited. There would be no outrunning the angels, not without my magic. And I didn't want to use that just yet. I needed them to see me disappear. Needed them to know I had left. But as we looked up to the sky, they passed us by. I looked at Castiel, who seemed equally confused.

"Where are they going?" I asked. He only shook his head.

"They're heading for the docks."

Oh. So, they figured out where he was staying, too.

"What do we do?" I asked. "Should we head down there? Confront them?"

"No, absolutely not." He sheathed his sword again and grabbed my arm. "We run."

"What happened to you fighting?"

"It's like you said, they're too many." He started walking, and I had no choice but to follow. "Until you get me my wings back, we're far too vulnerable here in the city. We'd be much safer in the country until we figure things out."

"Hold on!" I stopped him, digging my heels into the ground. Castiel barely seemed to notice the bit of resistance. "I can't leave without knowing that they won't go after my sisters."

"You might not have a choice."

"So, I just leave like a coward while my sisters are attacked for having the misfortune of knowing me?" I shook my head violently. "Absolutely not."

Castiel sighed and let go of my arm. "Then what? We seek them out? I don't know about you, but I wasn't planning on getting killed tonight."

I scoffed. "If you want to leave, then leave. But you'll be leaving without me *and* my magic."

"No, I'm not letting you out of my sight," he protested. "Are all witches this annoying?"

I shrugged. "I'm just special, I guess."

He rolled his eyes again. "Fine. We'll go to the docks and look into what's going on. But we do *not* instigate anything. I need to have my powers if we're to even stand a chance of making it out from a fight with that many angels."

"Hey," I said, "I have powers, too. I can get us out."

"Sure," he said. "If you say so."

I ignored the obvious sarcasm in his voice and started walking. Castiel soon caught up with me, and we kept one eye on the sky all the way to the docks. We found at least a dozen angels outside Castiel's hut, the front door ripped off its hinges. Castiel tensed beside me, and I quickly put a hand on his arm. It wouldn't stop him if he decided to do something about them invading his space, but it seemed to center him in reality—at least a little. He stayed hidden by my side as we crouched behind some metal crates.

"Keep looking."

There was no doubting who that booming voice belonged to. I saw Gabriel come out of the hut, flanked by two other angels. He was holding something in his hand, but I couldn't make out what it was. Castiel, however, seemed to know *exactly* what was in the archangel's hand.

And before I could stop him, he was running toward them all.

CHAPTER 5

"C astiel!" I hissed, keeping myself crouched down, but I was tempted to pull him back with a spell. It was too late, though. They had already spotted him. Hard not to when he started running at full speed, sword drawn.

"Damn it," I wheezed, and then chaos broke out. He attacked blindly, and two of the angels had him on the ground within seconds. I bit my lip. I could just run. Leave him there and get away while they were distracted. But then they might just go to the coven anyway, and... I couldn't just leave him here to be torn to shreds. So, with my blade in one hand and my magic at the ready, I stepped forward. Gabriel was the first to see me come, and a wicked grin spread across his lips.

"Danika," he said. "I get to see you again so soon! Lucky me."

"Call back your brothers," I said, inching closer to where Castiel lied on the ground, my blade raised in front of my body.

"And why should I do that?" he asked, throwing that thing up in the air, only to catch it again. I still didn't understand what it was. Some sort of metal box, or maybe it was stone. Either way, the black surface of the thing barely caught the light of the street lamp nearby; it was just too dark.

"Enough," I hissed, more to myself than to anyone else. I slashed at the angels that got in my way, but they simply jumped back, out of reach of my blade. Alright, then. It was apparently time for the heavier stuff.

I put my blade back inside my jacket; I wouldn't need it anymore. Pulling on my magic, I felt it course through me, the familiar electricity making the hairs stand on the back of my neck. Gabriel was watching me, amusement in his eyes. Like I was some child about to perform a trick she'd learned at school for her bored parent. With both hands raised to my side, I unleashed the spell. Chanting the ancient words, I felt the ground shudder beneath my feet.

Apparently, Gabriel felt it, too.

"Get her."

I grabbed hold of the first angel that came toward

me, pushing heat onto his skin until it burned. The next got nailed down to the ground before even laying a hand on me. I saw a flicker of uncertainty in Gabriel's eyes, but he wasn't my primary concern at the moment. Castiel's sword was a few feet away, and he was still being held down.

I just needed to get us out and put as much distance as I could between us and the others. I had to be quick about it, and I hoped Castiel would be quick, too. Taking one deep breath, I hoped I would have enough strength in me to pull what was about to happen off. My eyes met Castiel's for a fraction of a second, and then I slammed my clenched fists into the ground. My powers rushed through me, causing the asphalt to crack and break. It threw the angels to the ground, the moment of surprise enough to send them off balance. Castiel got onto his feet, lunging for his sword.

"Come on!" I yelled, trying to calm my beating heart.

"The box!" he yelled back. "I need that box."

Gabriel had spread his wings, and I almost let him fly. But one look at Castiel's desperate face told me that the box wasn't just some sentimental knick-knack. It was important.

So, just as the archangel took flight, I reached for him with my magic, tethering him to the ground. Gabriel released a furious cry, and I felt my arms start to shake with the effort of keeping him down. The other angels were getting back up, too. We *really* didn't have much time.

I yanked, making Gabriel flutter above us. I yanked again, making the elements push him down. I didn't have much left in me, and he was fighting me tooth and nail. But then Castiel stepped forward, and I yanked one last time.

This time, Gabriel lost his balance and dropped several feet. It was enough for Castiel to cut along the archangel's leg with his sword—as deep as he could at the awkward angle. It didn't seem to do as much damage as he might've intended, but it was enough to make Gabriel cry out and drop the box. Castiel caught it midair, and then he sprinted toward me.

"Behind the hut!" he cried out. "Go!"

I ran as fast as I could, following him as he sprinted down some stairs that were around the corner of his hut. A helicopter stood there. Just a small one, old as fuck, but if it could fly, it might just get us out of here. Once inside, Castiel flipped some of the switches on the dashboard, and the engine roared to life.

"You just have this standing here?" I asked, strapping myself in.

"I don't use it much, but I figure now is probably a good time to take it for a spin."

I really hoped the old thing could carry us far enough away; it looked like it might crash at any moment. I glanced over my shoulder through the back window and saw the angels following us.

"You're gonna need to go faster than this!" I cried out. "They're closing in on us!"

Castiel pushed a lever, and the engine sputtered to life, but at least we were moving faster. We moved further away from the docks. Further away from the city. In just a few short moments, the lights were just a distant thing from the sky.

I couldn't see the angels anymore, but they were most likely following us unless Gabriel had ordered them to stop. If he had, it wasn't because he had given up on finding us. They would come soon enough.

I was sure of it.

"You think they're gone?" I asked and turned back to the front, slumping in my seat. Castiel shook his head.

"Not likely. And if they are, they'll be coming back soon."

Just as I thought. At least they'd seen us fly out of the city together. Surely, that meant they weren't going to go back to my coven. If they did, I hoped Tatia would enact her revenge for what they did to Yvette. And then some.

"Do you have a plan of where we're going?" I asked. Castiel nodded.

"I know a place. We won't be able to stay for long, but it'll work for a day or two. It'll just take an hour or so to get there."

An hour with a heli like this? I prepared myself for an uncomfortable ride. Then I spotted the black metal box.

"What's so important about that thing that it was worth almost getting killed over?" I asked.

Castiel glanced down at the box sitting on his lap. "Don't worry about it."

"Did you seriously just tell me not to worry about it? I know we just met and all, but surely, you must know that it's not my style to not worry."

Castiel smirked. "Yeah, I kinda figured, but just trust me on this one. You don't need to know."

I frowned. "If I had known back there that the box was important, we could've made a plan instead of just blindly rushing in there. We almost got killed. There were about a dozen angels there, Castiel!"

He sighed. "I know, but we made it out. That's what's important."

"Yeah, no thanks to you."

He glanced over at me. "What do you want me to say? That I'm eternally grateful, thanks to the almighty witch. That I owe you big time?"

"Well, that's a start."

He scoffed and turned the steering levers to the right. We were getting further and further away from the city, and I looked back to see its tall buildings and the millions upon millions of lights.

I held onto my seat as the heli dropped a little. I turned to Castiel, my heart in my throat. "What the fuck was that?"

"It does that sometimes," he said and steered it back up again. "Nothing to worry about; we won't crash or anything."

I raised an eyebrow. "Why do you even have this thing. It's ancient."

"It's not ancient," he retorted. "It's vintage."

"Right. It's a cheap piece of crap that's going to get us killed, is what it is."

"You're more than welcome to walk, you know."

Yeah, no. I wasn't about to do that. So, I just narrowed my eyes at him, making sure he *knew* that I still thought the helicopter was in offensively bad shape, and then I turned my face forward, not saying another word.

After a while of looking straight ahead out through the front window, I saw that we were flying over a suburb of the city. The houses weren't as tall here, and there were gardens every once in a while. I knew from my grandfather's old pictures that there used to be a lot more of this. Grass, trees, even animals. I didn't think I'd ever seen a wild animal in my life. I knew they were out there; I just wasn't sure where.

"This place we're going to," I asked, breaking the long silence, "what is it?"

"When I first came here, this place was where I hid out during the day. It's just an abandoned cabin in the countryside."

When he first came here, meaning when he fell out of the sky, or when he met his human mate? I didn't bother asking. It wasn't important. I *was* a bit curious, though. Castiel was the first fallen angel I had ever met, and I definitely had questions for him. But that would have to wait until we reached the cabin.

The only sound for miles was the roar of the engine, which only seemed to get worse and worse the longer we flew. If we managed to go undetected in this thing, it would be nothing short of a miracle. We were going to have to ditch it as soon as we could and find some other way of getting around. It was just too loud.

It suddenly struck me how dark it was outside. The further we got from the city, the fewer artificial lights could be seen. I barely knew that darkness like this could even exist. There was always something illuminating my every step. Neon signs, streetlights, flashing lights at the different clubs downtown. But out here, it was just... dark. Quiet.

"I don't think I've ever been this far outside the city before," I mumbled quietly as if my voice would break something if I spoke too loud. Castiel looked surprised.

"You've never traveled outside the city?"

I shook my head. "No need. I have my coven there. Besides, everything I need is in the city."

"Sure, but there's a whole world out there," he said. "Haven't you ever wanted to see it?"

I shrugged. "I never gave it much thought."

Castiel made a humming sound deep in his throat. "Well, at least you'll see some of it now."

I huffed out a laugh. "Yeah, I doubt we'll see much, hiding away in abandoned houses."

"True," he agreed. "But at least you'll get to see the forest."

"It's in the forest? Won't there be wild animals there?"

There was that smirk again. "Why? Are you afraid of the little rabbits and foxes?"

"I wouldn't know," I said. "I've never seen any."

"You can't be serious."

"I grew up in the city, remember?" I shrugged. "Not a lot of rabbits or foxes around."

"I guess." Castiel checked something on the dashboard. "We should be there soon."

"When was the last time you were there?"

"A few years."

"What if it's gone?"

He gave me an irritated look. "It won't be gone."

"It could be gone," I pointed out. "The whole area could have been bought by developers, and now there are only luxury apartments out in the woods."

"Do you ever think back on all the things that come out of your mouth and wonder what was going on inside your head at that moment?" Castiel asked. "Because I sure do. There won't be any luxury cabins."

"Stranger things have happened."

He didn't answer.

The ride was over in the next fifteen minutes. We slowly descended, touching the ground in even denser darkness than before. I stepped outside, and the silence struck me like a slap to the face. Except it wasn't completely quiet. The more I listened, the more I heard. Little chirps from the birds. The rustling of leaves as the wind passed through the trees. In fact, it wasn't quiet at all.

And the trees were so *tall*. The trees back home

towered over me, sure. But these were something entirely different. They seemed endless!

"You really haven't seen the forest before, have you?"

I looked at Castiel, and there was something that seemed like amazement on his face. I shook my head. "I told you, I haven't."

"Yeah, but I just... It's strange seeing it through your eyes, I guess."

We left the heli standing there, and I wondered if it was going to get eaten by the forest if it stood there long enough. Probably. Castiel led me across a narrow trail, and I tripped several times over small rocks and roots that crossed the path.

"I can't see a thing," I said after I got back onto my feet after falling for the fourth time. "This is ridiculous!"

Before he could say anything, I conjured a spell and produced a small spark of light in the palm of my hand. The heat coursed through me, but I could handle it for a short while. Castiel nodded at the light.

"That's very practical."

"Magic has its perks."

With my hand raised, illuminating the path, we kept trekking through the woods. After a while, I saw the outlines of a house. The closer we got, the smaller it seemed. It was painted dark brown, and I noticed that the exterior was made entirely of wood. Interesting. I didn't think I'd ever see a house made of wood.

"This is it," Castiel said and stepped up to the front door.

Some of the windows had been smashed, but they were covered with plastic. The place was an absolute shithole, but I had imagined something far worse. I turned off my light and found that I could still see Castiel's face quite clearly.

There was a light coming from *somewhere*. From *inside* the cabin. Castiel seemed to realize the same thing.

"Strange," he said.

"Maybe it's an animal that turned on the lights," I suggested.

When Castiel gave me an exasperated look, I didn't blame him. The words had sounded stupid, even to my own ears.

Through the plastic covers over the closest window, I could suddenly hear humming. Castiel put a hand on the hilt of his sword when he heard it, too.

I swallowed.

"Someone is here."

We pressed ourselves up against the cabin wall. Castiel tried to look in through the closest window, but the plastic made things blurry.

"I saw movement," he said. "And he's still humming."

"What do we do?" I asked. "It's probably just a human."

He nodded. "Yeah, probably. But maybe we should move on."

"And go where? We can't keep traveling in that

heli of yours; it attracts too much attention! And we need a plan. A *real* plan."

"So, what do you suggest?" he snapped. "We just knock on the door and ask to stay?"

I chewed on my bottom lip, trying to think. "We can just say that we're lost or something. Ask to stay for a couple of nights. And besides, a human is not much of a threat to a witch and an angel."

"I don't have my powers, remember?"

"But you have your sword. I take it that works on humans as well?"

He rolled his eyes. "Of course it does." There was a pause, and then he nodded. "Okay. Let's do it. I guess it's our best option. But keep your blade ready."

I didn't take it out; it was enough to know that I had the blade on me. Castiel stood in front of the door, me right behind him. He raised his hand to knock when the door flung open. We backed up, and I saw Castiel's hand grip the hilt of his sword tightly. A young man stood there, eyes fixed on us.

"You guys aren't being *nearly* as quiet as you think you are."

Castiel and I exchanged a look. "Sorry," I said. "We weren't expecting anyone to be here."

"I've been here for months," the man said. "What is this? Some lovers' getaway in the woods? I'm telling you, there are hotels around if you're looking for that sort of thing. A lot more comfortable than this place."

"Who are you?" Castiel asked, and there was no

mistaking the edge in his voice. The stranger squared his shoulders.

"My name is Micah. And who are you? I like to at least know the names of the people barging in on me in the middle of the night."

"It's not important," Castiel said. "We need a place to stay for a day or two. Do you mind?"

"Not if you tell me your names. And maybe if you leave that thing at the door." Micah eyed Castiel's sword.

"My name is Danika," I said before Castiel could protest again. "This is Castiel. We wouldn't be here if it wasn't an emergency. We're just asking for one or two nights."

Micah's eyes traveled along the length of my body, and to my annoyance, I felt myself blush. There was something about the look he was giving me that made me squirm.

"Fine," he said. "You may come inside. But only for a few days. I can't have a bunch of people running around here like it's some kind of party."

"Only for a few days," I promised.

Micah stepped aside, and we walked through the door. I noticed that he was almost as tall as Castiel, a feat in and of itself, and there was something else that seemed off about him. Then I realized. Standing in front of Micah, I looked at his blue eyes.

"You're a Nephila!"

His face hardened. "Say it louder, will ya? It's not like there are angels out there or anything."

Castiel frowned. "Is that why you're hiding out here? You got on the angels' radar?"

Micah nodded. "That's right. Is that why you came out here? You're obviously Nephilim, too." He eyed Castiel, and the angel shook his head.

"I'm not Nephilim."

"He's fallen," I filled in. Micah's eyes widened.

"Fallen?" He backed up a step. "So, you are one of them!"

"Don't worry," Castiel assured him. "I do not share my former brothers' views on your kind."

"If you say so." Micah turned his focus back to me. "And what about you? Why does a human go hide out in the woods with a fallen angel?"

"She's a witch," Castiel said before I could open my mouth.

"A witch?" Micah asked. "I haven't met one of your kind in a really long time. And the ones I knew were all old crones. Clearly, that's not the case with every one of your kind." A smile spread across his lips, a twinkle in those blue eyes. I rolled my eyes, but I couldn't stop the small smile that tugged at my lips. I caught a glimpse of Castiel's face and was surprised at the annoyance I saw there.

"You said the angels are out there," I said to Micah, trying to bring back the conversation to what mattered. "Have you seen them in the area?"

Micah nodded. "They haven't found this place yet; they tend to keep to the cities. But yeah, I've seen them fly past here at night. I'm surprised you didn't see any out there."

Castiel looked over to me, and I glanced back. We'd been lucky, then. I didn't remember seeing any angels in the sky once we landed.

"You said you'd been here for months?" I asked. "Why don't you look into other options? There are ways to free yourself. Ways to get the angels to stop noticing you."

"She can help you," Castiel said and nodded at me. "She has helped many Nephilim become free."

"By stripping them of all that makes them who they are, no doubt," Micah taunted. "Thanks, but no."

"You wouldn't want to live your life in peace?" I asked. "As a human?"

"Absolutely not," Micah said. "I am not human; I am Nephilim. Until we fight back, we will just keep getting killed. I know many just want to live without fear, but I'm not afraid. So, I'll be keeping my powers."

"Okay," I replied. "You are choosing a difficult life, but the choice is still yours."

"It is. Thank you, though." There was a pause, and I felt Micah's eyes on me again. I kept my gaze on Castiel, not sure what to do with the attention from the Nephila. After a while though, I couldn't hold my tongue.

"Do I have something on my face?"

A grin spread across his face. "I'm sorry. I was just thinking."

"Don't strain yourself."

"You offered your help so willingly," he said, ignoring my comment. "If you offered it to the wrong person, things could get bad. Sure, most Nephilim want nothing to do with the angels, but there are a few that work with them."

"I'd say the angels have their eyes on me regardless of who I help," I told him. "But thanks for your concern."

"Just saying," he said. "Not everyone is as innocent as they seem."

"You could say that again," Castiel muttered and sank down onto one of the chairs by the raggedy kitchen table. "Who sired you?"

Micah jerked a little at the intrusive question, and I glared at Castiel, willing him to shut up.

"I do not know my sire," Micah said. "My mother never talked about him."

Castiel hummed, obviously not believing him. I didn't see any reason for Micah to lie, though. But maybe Castiel still carried some sort of mistrust for the Nephilim, despite what he said about supporting their existence.

"We should probably get some rest," I said, steering the conversation away from anything controversial. "If the angels were to show up, we'll need our strength."

"There's room on my bed," Micah said with a wink. Castiel stood up, his chair toppling over onto the wooden floor.

"We'll take the couch," he said, leaving no room for discussion.

Micah winked at me again, an amused look on his face. He leaned in close and whispered into my ear. "If it gets too crowded, the offer still stands."

I shook my head. "The couch is fine." *Cheeky bastard.* Micah nodded and looked at Castiel's sword again.

"And I meant it when I said the sword should be kept by the door. We wouldn't want any accidents, now would we?"

Castiel glared at him as he left the room, probably disappearing off into the bedroom. I couldn't help but laugh at the look on his face.

"You find this amusing?" Castiel asked, taking off his belt with the sword attached to it. "Or are you so easily charmed?"

"Oh, I'm a simple girl," I said and shrugged off my jacket. "All I need are some smiles and twinkling eyes, and of course, the pleasure of watching you get so flustered when getting bossed around."

"He did *not* boss me around," Castiel insisted.

"You've taken off your sword, haven't you?"

He didn't respond. I smiled and turned to the couch. It was a massive thing, thankfully, stretching across almost the entire wall of the room. We'd both fit without issue. I grabbed one of the blankets that were draped over the armrest and got comfortable.

"So," I began, "what are we going to do now? We might be able to stay for a day or two, but not much longer."

"Yes, that's a nuisance," Castiel huffed as he sat

down on the other end of the couch. He glanced toward the bedroom at the nuisance in question. "I was hoping we could get everything sorted here with my wings and my powers. But it doesn't seem wise with the Nephila around." He chewed on his lip, thinking. "There is another city fairly close to here. We could go there. Hide amongst the crowd until we find someplace more remote again."

I nodded and pulled the blanket up to my chin. "That could work. How far is it?"

"With the helicopter…"

"We're *not* taking the heli!"

"Fine. If we travel on foot, I guess it would take us a couple of days to get there."

"A couple of days?!" I asked. "I thought you said it was close."

"Relatively close," he replied. "We are quite far out here."

"Okay, I guess we don't have any other options," I said. "I just think that maybe…"

I paused, temporarily dumbstruck when Castiel took off his shirt and threw it to the ground. He didn't seem to notice me staring, just got under a blanket of his own and leaned back on the couch. I swallowed, my cheeks burning.

I knew he'd be built; it was hard not to notice even when he was fully clothed. But *damn*. He really *was* sculpted from Heaven.

"You got awfully quiet," he said, sounding annoyingly cheery. Okay, maybe he *did* notice me staring. I closed my eyes, willing my body to disappear through the floor.

"Shut up."

A low chuckle rumbled in his chest, and I could feel the warmth from his body as he shifted in his spot. Our feet were close enough to touch, so I pulled my legs closer to myself and made sure to stick to my side.

I should've just gone with Micah. I knew he was flirting, but I was sure he wouldn't have actually done anything if I didn't want to. He seemed nice.

I rolled over onto my side, not finding a comfortable position to fall asleep in. The couch was old and worn out, and the cushioning wasn't exactly something to write home about.

"Will you stop that?" Castiel huffed, his voice low as to not wake Micah.

"This is the most uncomfortable couch in the history of couches."

"Well, I'm sorry it's not some five-star hotel. Just... relax."

"You relax!" I snapped back.

"Kinda difficult when you're bouncing around like that."

"I rolled over *once*. Get over it."

He didn't say anything for a moment. Then I rolled over again, and a giant sigh escaped him. "Seriously?"

I sat up. "I can go sleep in the bedroom if you have a problem."

Castiel sat up, too, the blanket pooling at his waist. I did *not* look. "No," he said quickly.

"Why not? You'd get the whole couch to yourself."

"*No.*"

I smirked. "Okay, then."

Lying back down, I immediately started to roll this way and that. I glanced over at him and snickered when I saw him glaring at me. But he didn't say anything else, just lied back down also, arms crossed over his chest, and closed his eyes.

CHAPTER 7

I woke up early, well before Castiel. It was still dark outside. I couldn't have slept more than an hour or two. But I felt wide awake; the stillness of the forest outside unnerved me somehow. I was so used to all the sounds in the city that it was hard to just hear... nothing.

I needed to pee and carefully got out from under my blanket. I stilled for a moment when Castiel made a noise, but as soon as I was sure I hadn't woken him up, I started to search for a toilet. Once I had done my business, I returned to the small living room. There was a jittery sort of feeling running through me, and I knew I wouldn't be able to fall back asleep. I needed to think.

Carefully opening the front door, I snuck outside. I just needed some air, so I sat down on the front steps, looking out at the forest. The air felt different out there than what I was used to back in the city. It was probably cleaner without all the trains and the ships from the docks, but I wasn't so sure I liked it.

Strange, maybe. But I had grown up in the city and was used to the smells and sounds that came with it. I had lived in both the good and bad parts, being born in simple conditions and climbed up in the ranks as my magic grew. I thought about my grandfather who had taken me in after my parents were gone. I remembered the humble apartment down by the canal and the old bed where I used to sleep. It was all I needed.

He kept me entertained with his stories about his own childhood, about the time before the angels had come to terrorize our community. There had been the occasional angel, of course, even in his childhood. But there had been no curfew at night. There had barely been any Nephilim. Not like these days.

I wondered why that was. The angels were far older than my grandfather had been. Why had some of them started to come down over the past few decades? Having children who would undoubtedly be killed. Risk meeting the same fate as Castiel had.

I wondered how many more fallen angels walked the Earth. Did they also want to return, like Castiel? I couldn't understand why. Sure, Heaven was their home, but what sort of life could they have there? Surely, they couldn't just return and expect their brothers to have any sort of warm feelings toward them. The fallen were shunned, cast out of Heaven.

I glanced behind me at the shut door. I wondered what Castiel's real reason was for wanting to return. Because I very much doubted that it was just a matter of homesickness.

When the door opened, I almost jumped out of my skin. I relaxed again when Micah peeked his head out.

"I thought I heard someone go outside," he said and walked through the door. He carefully closed it again and looked down at me. "Mind if I join you?"

I shook my head. "No, not at all."

He sat right next to me on the steps, our legs pressing together. He looked a bit different out here in the quiet night. The teasing look had gone from his face. He seemed more... genuine.

"You couldn't sleep either?" I asked, and he shook his head.

"I'm not used to having people around. Every noise makes me jump."

"Sorry. We didn't know anyone would be here."

He turned his face to me and smiled. "No, I know. Really, it's no trouble. I'm glad for the company." A small chuckle escaped him. "Although I don't think the big guy likes me very much."

I smiled. "I don't know him very well, so I can't

pretend to know what he feels. But he has been through a lot. I don't think he trusts very easily."

"He trusts you," Micah said.

"I don't know." I started picking at the edge of my shirt. "He needs something from me. That's different."

The Nephila nodded and looked back out at the forest surrounding us. "Maybe. Regardless, he doesn't like me."

I huffed out a quiet laugh. "Why do you say that?"

Micah looked at me again, some of the teasing look back on his face. "Because I was flirting with you."

To my annoyance, I felt my face go hot. "You were not flirting with me." *Yes, he was.*

"Oh, yeah, I definitely was," he said. "Wasn't it obvious? Maybe I've been out here too long by myself. I clearly need to brush up on my skills if you didn't notice."

It wasn't that I hadn't noticed, I just didn't take it seriously. It wasn't something I was used to. I was much too busy with my coven to even entertain the idea of romance. Not that I was entirely inexperienced, but that was beside the point. Not many people flirted with me, but apparently, Micah had been serious with his teasing remarks. I wasn't sure what to do with that information.

"Look," he said and smirked. "I'm sorry if I've made you uncomfortable. Don't worry, I'm harmless."

"I'm not worried," I lied.

"Good." Micah's gaze fell from my eyes to my lips. "Because my offer still stands."

"Your offer?"

His smirk widened. "In case that couch is too uncomfortable or... crowded. There are other places for you to sleep."

I shook my head. He certainly wasn't afraid to put his intentions out there. Micah was good-looking with his blonde hair and striking eyes. His body was strong and lean, and under any other circumstance, I might have considered going back to his bedroom with him. But now... I glanced back at the door again.

"The couch is fine," I said.

He nodded. "The choice is yours entirely. I won't push the issue again, I promise." He bumped my shoulder lightly. "But I might not be able to resist *some* flirting. It's much too fun watching the angel in there turn all red in the face when I get too close to you."

"Don't be ridiculous; he doesn't care about that," I said. Micah scoffed.

"If you say so."

He got back up onto his feet and went back inside. I pulled my arms around myself. It was getting kind of cold.

When I walked back inside, the door to Micah's room was closed. He must've gone back to bed. I walked over to the couch and lied down. As I pulled the blanket over my body, Castiel stirred.

"Are you awake?" he whispered and pushed himself up onto his elbows. The faint light from the moon outside cast a beautiful glow on his skin. The swell of his muscled arms was that much more noticeable than it usually was, and I felt my heart pick up its pace. *Stop staring at him*, I mentally scolded myself.

"I couldn't sleep," I said. "I just went outside for some air."

Castiel cast a look at Micah's door. "Did he join you?"

"For a short while, yes."

He made a noise in his throat but didn't push on. "Don't let him get in your head."

I half sat up, too. "What's that supposed to mean?"

"He's flirting with you," Castiel explained as if that was enough of an answer. I raised a brow at him.

"So, what if he is? I'm a grown woman. I don't need you hovering over me like you're my father or something."

Castiel scowled. "I'm just saying, just because someone is charming doesn't mean they have your best interest at heart."

"Micah has taken us in despite the fact that you're an angel," I pointed out. "He has been nothing but respectful to me. You're seeing a threat where there is none." I lied back down with a huff. "And I still don't understand why it's a bad thing if someone is flirting with me."

He didn't say anything more after that. Just lied down also and stared up at the ceiling. I shook my head; Castiel was being ridiculous! Besides, it wasn't like I couldn't handle myself. I had fought against angels and archangels my whole life and lived to tell the tale. I could handle one flirtatious Nephila. I peeked one eye open and looked at Castiel. His eyes were closed, but he was clearly still awake. His arms were crossed over his chest, and there was a sort of tension in his jaw, making him look pretty pissed off.

I didn't sleep any more that night. I suspected Castiel didn't either.

CHAPTER 8

Micah prepared a simple breakfast for us when the morning finally came, and I scarfed it down like I had never seen food before. I couldn't even find it in myself to be embarrassed; I was just so hungry. It was some sort of sweet porridge, and it was amazing!

"Happy to see that my cooking is appreciated," he said with a laugh. I smiled at him, ignoring the way that Castiel looked at me.

"Thank you for this. We were lucky to find you out here."

Micah opened his mouth to answer, but Castiel cut in before he got the chance. "Why *are* you out here, anyway?"

"I told you before," Micah said and took a sip of his tea. "I got on the angels' radar."

"But how did you get on their radar to begin with?" Castiel pressed on. "What did you do?"

"Castiel, stop it. Seriously!" I hissed at him, but he ignored me.

"What did I do?" Micah repeated, an edge to his voice. "What did any of us do? I'm Nephilim. I was *born*. That's enough to put a target on my back."

"But you've been out here for months, hiding. You must've really pissed them off."

One of the corners of Micah's mouth lifted. "I might have caused a bit of trouble."

Castiel huffed out a breath. "Why do I not have a hard time believing that?"

Micah and I exchanged a look. "If you must know, I stole something from one of them."

"You stole from the angels?" I asked, not sure if I should laugh or be horrified. "Was it something valuable?"

Micah looked at me like that was an incredibly stupid question. "Of course, it was valuable. But that's also why I'm a bit *more* on their radar than the average Nephila might be."

"What did you take?" Castiel asked. I could've been wrong, but I thought he looked a tiny bit impressed.

"I took a sword," Micah said casually and nodded at Castiel's sword that was leaning against the wall. "Just like that one."

Castiel raised his eyebrows at him. "You took an angel's sword?"

"I did." Micah nodded. "He wasn't very happy about it."

"How in the world did you manage to get away?" I asked. Micah shrugged.

"He was badly injured. I guess I got lucky."

"Do you know how to use it?" Castiel asked, popping the last bit of his bread into his mouth.

"I know not to touch the sharp bit at the end, if that's what you're asking."

Castiel rolled his eyes. "Do you always have to be such a smartass?"

"It *is* one of my finest traits, so yes."

"Do you know how to *use* it?" he repeated.

"I haven't had any training, no."

"Go and get it, and meet me outside," Castiel ordered. "I'll show you."

"You will?" Micah asked. "If you stab me, Danika will avenge me."

"Of course!" I exclaimed. "Go on. I wanna see this."

He got up, still not looking entirely convinced that Castiel actually wanted to show him how to use the sword. When he was no longer within earshot, I turned to Castiel.

"You're very charitable today. Just last night, you warned me against him."

"I decided that you're right," Castiel said and got up from his chair. "He took us in, and this is my way of repaying that kindness. If he has a sword, he should know how to use it."

"And if you slip and run him through, that's just an unfortunate accident, right?"

Castiel smiled. "I don't intend to run him through. He might get cut, but that's just unavoidable when training with real weapons."

I got up with him and gave him a look. "I'm sure."

Castiel grabbed my arm and smirked at me. "I might even have to take off my shirt. It's a warm day."

Oh, he loved watching me squirm, the asshole. "Why do you think I care?"

"Oh, I don't know," Castiel teased. "You seemed to enjoy yourself last night before bed."

My treacherous cheeks burned bright red. "You certainly think highly of yourself, don't you?"

Castiel didn't answer. Just chuckled and let go of my arm. A minute later, Micah rejoined us. He was carrying a sword that looked almost identical to the one that Castiel carried.

"Let me see that," Castiel said and reached for the weapon. Micah handed it to him.

"The angel's name was Malakh. Do you know him?

Castiel shook his head, his brow furrowed as he

inspected the sword. "I don't think I do, but based on the carvings here, he must've been pretty high up in the ranks." He showed us the hilt of the sword, where the surface had been carved in an ornate pattern. "He might've even been working directly under one of the archangels. They have similar markings on their swords."

Micah gave a low whistle. "So, you're saying I stole from one of the big boys. Good to know."

"I'm honestly surprised you're not dead yet for this alone," Castiel muttered. "Not to mention the fact that you're Nephilim."

"What can I say?" Micah exclaimed and grinned. "I'm resourceful."

"Clearly." Castiel handed the sword back to him. "Let's go outside. I'll show you the basics."

We both followed him outside, and he grabbed his own sword on the way out. There was an open space right in front of the cabin, and Castiel chose it as their training spot. I sat down on the stairs, just as I had during the night, and watched them get started.

Castiel positioned Micah in a fighting stance and had him try out some moves. They worked slowly, but I suspected that with enough speed and strength, those moves could be deadly. After an hour of running through the moves, Castiel suggested that they put Micah to the test. I straightened when the two men stood opposite each other, weapons raised. This was going to be interesting.

"Remember," Castiel repeated, "focus on

protecting yourself rather than attacking. You're only as strong as your defenses."

When Micah nodded, Castiel started right away. In one swift move, he had his opponent's sword on the ground, and Micah was left without a weapon. The Nephila's face turned red, and he bent down to pick up the sword.

"Again," he said through gritted teeth.

"You need to parry with a lot more power than that," Castiel said. "Every blow will be backed up with all of your opponent's strength. You need to be able to meet that without dropping your weapon."

"Yeah, yeah." Micah brushed him off. "Go again."

This time, Micah managed to hold his own for at least a minute before Castiel had his sword against his throat. "You're leaving yourself too open. Remember, protect yourself."

"Got it. Again."

They went back and forth for the better part of the next two hours. Both men were covered in sweat, and despite not being evenly matched, Micah got better and better with each blow. I rested my chin on the palm of my hand as I watched, and Micah grinned.

"Are you enjoying the show?"

I laughed. "Immensely. Although, I was told there'd be shirtless men involved."

At my words, Castiel glanced my way. I noticed the corner of his mouth curving up in a smile, and I grinned. I might've been a bit embarrassed before, but out here in the open, it didn't seem quite as... intimate.

They carried on for a while longer before Micah put an end to the session.

"My arm might fall off if we do anymore," he said. "And I need my arm. My favorite hand is attached to it."

Castiel shook his head at the bad joke and dragged a hand over his sweaty face. He looked over at me, and a smile spread across his lips. In one strong move, he jabbed the sword into the ground, and then he grabbed the hem of his shirt and pulled it over his head. I couldn't help but laugh when he made a big show of wiping his forehead with the shirt.

Well, if he was putting himself on display, I wasn't going to look away. I heard Micah laugh, too, as he walked over to me.

"There. The promise has been fulfilled," he said and clapped me on the shoulder. I stood up as he went inside and turned to Castiel.

"If you're done flexing, you should come inside." We had been out here for most of the day, and the sun was beginning to set. Best to get out of the open before dark.

Castiel walked up to me, his shirt still slung over his shoulder. "We leave tomorrow," he whispered quietly as if he didn't want Micah to hear. "Now he'll at least be able to fight if the angels find him."

I nodded. "Alright." We were almost at eye level with me standing on the steps. If I had wanted to, I could've just leaned forward and...

"Danika?"

I blinked. "Hm?"

"You're kinda blocking the way in."

I shuffled to the side. "Oh, right. Sorry."

He walked past me but stopped before he reached the door. "Aren't you coming?"

"In a minute," I said. "I just need some air."

"I can put my shirt back on if that helps," he teased, grinning wide.

I glared at him. "Just go inside."

His laughter echoed in my ears for several minutes after he left me standing there. I took one deep breath after another, and then I opened the door. There was no need to get so flustered. He was just a man.

A broad-shouldered, muscled, shirtless man.

I really was *pathetic*.

CHAPTER 9

The early morning sun shone through the windows, even the ones covered in plastic. I yawned, blinking as reality set in. I had slept so well last night, and I wasn't ready for the day to start yet. I didn't have much of a choice, though. Castiel was already up and dressed with his sword strapped to his side. I sat up, dragging a hand through my hair.

"Good morning," I said. "Is Micah—"

Castiel put a finger to his mouth, urging me to be quiet. I snapped my lips together, glancing at the closed bedroom door. Fine. Seemed like he wanted us to go before our host woke up. I guessed that was for the best. The fewer who knew where we were going, the better. And I didn't feel so bad leaving now that I knew Micah knew how to use his sword. I hoped he wouldn't be *too* offended that we just took off.

I got up, pulling on my boots and jacket. Castiel was waiting for me, standing by the door. As soon as I started moving toward him, he opened it up and stepped outside.

"Someone's eager to get away," I said, smacking my lips. I was thirsty, and my stomach growled with hunger. "It wouldn't have killed us to stick around for breakfast at least."

"I'll get you some breakfast later," he said, placing a hand on my lower back, moving me along.

"From one of the many cafés around here?"

"I can get you a river sludge latte if you're nice."

He let his hand fall from my back and took the lead. I scowled at him, tempted to stay put just to irk him. Making sure my blade was where it should be, and with one last look at the cabin, I hurried after him. The trail was even narrower here than where we had walked the day before, but at least the daylight prevented me from tripping over any roots this time around.

We walked in silence, and after a while, my legs were burning. I really wished I had a teleportation spell; it would've made my life so much easier. But since I didn't, I was just going to have to keep walking.

"Can I ask you a question?" I asked after a while. Castiel looked over his shoulder at me.

"Sure."

"How long have you been down here? Like this, I mean."

"I fell eight years ago," he said.

"Wow, eight years." I scowled. "Wait, how old are you? You couldn't have been more than a teenager if you fell eight years ago."

"We don't age like humans do," he explained. I knew that, but I didn't think it applied to fallen angels, too. Castiel continued. "I've aged slightly since they took my wings, but there is still angel blood in my veins. I suppose I'm somewhere around twenty-six in your years. Give or take a year or two."

"And in *your* years?"

He winked. "A bit older."

Yeah, that's what I thought. "What was it like? Heaven."

Castiel didn't answer right away. I saw the tension in his shoulders, and if I could've seen his face, I'm sure I would've seen it there, too. "It's a battlefield."

His answer surprised me. "Not exactly the image we have down here."

"No." He slowed down a little as the path became a bit wider, and I fell into step with him. "Heaven is..." He looked toward the sky as if trying to find the right words. "Heaven *was* what you'd think of it. Not anymore."

"What do you mean?"

"It's hard to explain," he said. "In many ways, it *is* like that. It's *Heaven*. But when you get into the core of it all, it's just a messed-up powerplay. A battle to have the most power, the most influence. A battle to eradicate that which isn't pure."

"Like the Nephilim."

"Exactly. Almost no humans ascend to Heaven after they die, and there haven't been any new angels for centuries. In fact, I believe I was one of the newer recruits."

"So, it's the same old farts fighting for power and outdated ideas of what's right and pure that run the show?" I made a face. "Sounds like the human leaders and the angels have a few things in common."

"Your leaders are fluffy little lambs compared to the angels," Castiel said.

"And yet, you want to rejoin their forces."

He looked over at me, his expression serious. "If you'd been stripped of your powers, would you not want them back?"

I shrugged. When he put it that way... "Of course, I would."

"Then why wouldn't I? I'm an angel, exiled from my people because I fell in love with someone they deemed off-limits. I do not plan on spending the rest of my days on Earth, accepting that fate."

"I suppose I can understand that. But I'm not sure if I can help you, Castiel. I've never done something like that before."

"I've seen you strip Nephilim of their powers," he

said. "I believe the process is similar." When he saw the doubt still on my face, he turned to me and placed a hand on my shoulder. "I chose to come to you for a reason. Trust me, if I didn't think you could do it, I wouldn't have asked."

"But why should I add to Heaven's numbers? Why should I put one more angel in the sky after everything your kind has done to mine? After the effect your mere presence has had on the city I call home."

"I'll pay you."

It was such a direct and simple solution that I almost laughed. "Oh, sure. Let me just cash in while everyone else is forced to stay inside at night because of your kind. Let me just make some credits while the angels are getting more and more intrusive in our world. Great idea."

I started to walk again, feeling him right behind me. "You know I'm not like that."

"I don't actually know you, Castiel."

"So, get to know me."

I felt him grab my hand. Gently, like he was gripping something fragile. I stopped and turned to look at him. "What?"

"Get to know me," he repeated. "And then you'll know that I'm not like them. We've spent several days together already. It hasn't been all bad, right?"

I didn't know what to say. He'd been alright, I'll admit. He had his moments for sure. But I still saw traits here and there that reminded me of the angels. I did believe that Castiel had good intentions. I *had* seen him help Micah, and he *did* looked after me. But that didn't change the fact that Heaven didn't need another angel to add to their forces. "I don't know."

"Danika, I need you." He stroked his thumb over the back of my hand. "No one else will help me. You are a good person. You go against your coven to help the Nephilim because it's the right thing to do. You came for me when I lost sight of things back at my hut. You are good. Will you really not help me?"

I narrowed my eyes at him. "You're a real charmer, you know that?"

"I'm not trying to charm you. I really mean it." Castiel let go of my hand and sighed. "I've watched you for a while."

"Creepy."

A hint of a smile curved his lips. "Maybe a little. But my point is that I came to you because I really believed that you'd help me."

He really put a lot on my shoulders. I still wasn't sure I was going to actually be able to do anything about his situation. And he could keep his credits; I didn't need them. But there might be something else I wanted. Information. I crossed my arms over my chest and looked at him.

"What's in the box?"

"What?"

"What's in the box?" I asked again. "You want my help? That's my price. I want to know what's in the box."

"I can't tell you that."

I pursed my lips and crossed my arms across my chest. "You going after that thing almost got both of us killed. If I'm going to go through the risk of restoring your wings and your powers, then I deserve to know."

"I'm sorry. I can't talk about it."

"Alright, then." I turned around and started walking again. It took a minute before I heard Castiel's footsteps behind me, but he soon caught up.

"You're just accepting that?" he asked. I shrugged.

"You'll tell me eventually."

"No, I won't."

"We'll see." I quickened my pace, not pressing the issue further. I *was* going to find out what was inside the box.

We both didn't say anything for a while, and when the sun was high in the sky, I broke the silence, wiping the sweat from my brow.

"You promised me breakfast. I'm fucking dying over here."

"Alright," Castiel said and walked past me. "I hear water. Let's go see what we can find."

The water turned out to be a small lake. I bent down and touched the water. It was cool to the touch, and it probably wouldn't be horrible for a swim. Oh, a swim sounded so nice after hours and hours of walking. But no. I wasn't about to strip naked in the middle of the forest in front of Mr. Vogue over there.

"There are some berries over here," Castiel called out to me a bit away. "Have some of those, and I'll see if I can find something more substantial."

"Are you sure they're safe to eat?" I asked and plucked one of the red berries from the bush.

"Yeah, they're a little tart, but they're perfectly safe. Wait here."

I popped the berry into my mouth as he ran off into the trees. He was right. The berry was almost sour, but after a few of them, they didn't taste so bad. I plucked a handful, then sat by the water and looked around. It was so beautiful, so *calm*.

When I finished the berries, I washed my hand in the lake, but my palms had already been stained red. Soon, Castiel returned with a long stick in his hand.

"You're going hunting?" I asked, smiling at the thought. Castiel shrugged.

"I thought I'd try my hand at fishing." He reached a hand out to me. "Can I use your blade for a bit?"

I reached into my jacket and handed it to him. The blade was so much smaller in his hand, but it worked well for carving the stick into a sharp point. When he was satisfied, he gave me back my weapon.

"How do you even know how to do this?" I asked. I didn't know anyone who did things like this, even though I knew that was how it was done. The stores didn't just magically grow fish. But there was something so *primal* about watching him roll his pants up and step out into the water, his makeshift spear raised.

"I *don't* know how to do this," he said. "But it seems logical that if you put a sharp stick into something, it might stay on said stick."

Fair enough. I sat there, watching as he poked the

stick in the water time after time again. Not one fish was on the other end of that spear. "We might as well just let Gabriel have me," I said when he pulled up an empty spear once again. "I'll die of starvation anyway."

"You do it then, if you think it's so easy," Castiel said and stuck the spear out to me. I laughed, then stood and tore my boots off. I rolled my pants up and joined him in the water. The stick was rough and coarse against my hand, but I gripped it tight anyway. At first, I didn't see any movement in the dark water, but after a while, I started to see the outlines of the fish under the surface. I zeroed in on one in particular and struck. Water splashed all over me, but there was no fish when I brought the stick back up. Castiel was sporting a particularly smug grin at that moment.

"Told you," he said.

"I'll try again," I snapped back, turning my gaze back to the water. The fish were swimming around our feet as if we just hadn't tried to kill them several times. I raised one hand over the surface, palm down. I whispered some words while I pulled on my magic. Making the water slow its current, the fish slowed down as well. Then I struck. This time, I was successful.

"Magic is cheating," Castiel complained.

"Not when you're as hungry as me." I handed him the spear back and started trudging through the water. "I'll start a fire."

CHAPTER 10

We didn't stay by the lake for long. With our bellies full of the fatty fish, we had some strength to continue on. The problem was that it was getting darker outside, and we were still a day's walk from our goal. The trees didn't stand as close together, and soon, we reached an actual road.

"We must be close to some sort of town," Castiel said. He gazed along the road. "I think I see lights further ahead."

"We should probably see if there's a place to sleep

tonight," I said. "I don't want to sleep outside when it's dark." He nodded, and I tried to ignore the blisters that had started to form under my feet as we walked along the road. Easier said than done. I was going to have to take care of that once we stopped for the night. After only a minute, Castiel stopped and grabbed my arm to get me to stop as well. He looked toward the sky, a worried expression on his face.

"What is it?" I asked and looked up, too. He didn't answer. He didn't have to.

Angels. Whether it was Gabriel and his brothers, I couldn't say. But regardless, I wasn't too keen on meeting any of them. We were both dressed in dark colors, so hopefully, they wouldn't see us. But it was still risky being out in the open like this.

"Should we go back into the woods?" I whispered.

Castiel shook his head. "No, I think they're just passing through. Keep going, but stay quiet."

Well, *duh*. I wanted to take out my blade but didn't want to risk it catching the faint light of the moon, exposing us. We walked slowly, always with one eye to the sky. I whispered the ancient words, hoping to shield us from view. But I couldn't focus, and the spell didn't take as I wanted it to.

After a while, Castiel just told me to leave it alone. It wouldn't help us for long anyway if they discovered us. So, we kept going. What other choice did we have? Besides, they were probably not going to see us; they were already pretty far off in the distance. But until they were out of sight completely, I wouldn't be able to relax. I hoisted my bag up onto my shoulder every few minutes as it kept sliding down. After a while, Castiel simply took it from me and slung it across his body.

"Thanks," I said, keeping my voice low.

"Don't worry about it." He suddenly tensed up. "Stop for a second."

"What is it?"

He hushed me, throwing an arm out in front of me, his eyes fixed on something further down the road. Then I saw it, too. Three large angels. The ones in the sky must've been set to get us to lower our guard, to make us believe they weren't aware of us. But of course, they were.

"Castiel." The angel in front nodded to him; they obviously knew each other. "So, it's true. You're still alive."

"And you still have your head up Gabriel's ass, I see, Cadriel," Castiel said, his voice rough like gravel. "Because I assume you are here on his behalf?"

"Come now," the angel, Cadriel, said. He wore an amused smile that barely reached his eyes. "Don't be like that."

Castiel placed himself slightly in front of me, his focus never leaving the three angels. "What do you want?"

"You killed two of my brothers, Castiel. *Your* former brothers. You know Gabriel doesn't take lightly on things like that." Cadriel's eyes shifted and looked at me. "And you're protecting *her*."

Castiel unsheathed his sword, the steel singing as he pulled it forth. "Your point being?"

"She aids the Nephilim."

"As she should." Castiel looked with utter disgust at the other angels. "The Nephilim have done nothing to you. To any of us."

Anger flashed across Cadriel's face. "I see your views on the matter haven't changed, even after so many years on Earth. Honestly, I don't know how you can stand it. Being among the humans." Then that smile returned. "But of course. How forgetful of me! You love the humans, don't you? Love them enough to fuc—"

"One more word," Castiel spat out, rushing forward a few steps. "One more word, and I'll rip out your tongue."

Cadriel clasped his hands in front of him and tilted his head as if he were watching an amusing little play. "Sensitive subject, huh? My apologies; it was insensitive of me. Remind me, what was her name? Sarah? Sophia?"

"Sydney."

He spoke the name so softly, so quietly. But there was strength in that name. A strength that made him stand taller and grip his weapon even tighter. I watched him, trying to imagine the man he had been with her. *Sydney*. He must've loved her very much.

I gripped my blade.

" Sydney," Cadriel exclaimed. "Of course. Such a

pretty little thing. Do you still visit her grave? Surely, you gave her one, for what was left of her anyway."

I acted without thinking. Clenching my hands together in front of my body and feeling the magic surge through my veins, I willed him to *shut up*. Closing off the air from passing through his throat, I made Cadriel cough and sputter.

Castiel was halfway over there, looking about ready to murder him when he stopped in his tracks and whirled around to face me. He must have sensed the rage I felt on his behalf because he smiled, a wicked smile that shook me to my core. Then he turned toward them again, sword raised. He struck Cadriel down before the other two could even blink.

Then shit broke loose.

The others parried, raising their own swords as Castiel attacked them, too. I rushed forward, doing my best to block them with my magic, but it was difficult when they were all moving so quickly. I didn't want to accidentally block Castiel.

One of them turned to me, his eyes burning with disdain. I didn't hesitate and slashed at him with my weapon once he was close enough. He roared when I sliced him across his abdomen, but it wasn't enough to bring him to his knees.

Instead, I just angered him further. Before I could get the words out to stop him, he had his strong hand wrapped around my neck. I clawed at him, trying to burn his skin, but it wasn't very effective when I couldn't speak to get the spell to work.

He tore the blade from my hand, throwing it to the ground. *Fuck.* Stripped of all my weapons, I started to kick. It barely seemed to faze him. He just tightened his grip on me, and black dots started dancing across the edges of my vision. I could hear Castiel and the other angel fighting somewhere behind me, but it was like listening through water. Distant and muddy. I clawed at his hand, needing it off of me.

"How fragile you are," the angel said, his voice soft like butter. "Even you, a witch. You're just a little human when you no longer have use of your powers, aren't you? How easy it is to simply squeeze the life right out of those strange, dark eyes of yours."

He squeezed some more for good measure, and I tried to kick him again. I couldn't muster the energy, though, and I felt reality slipping away from me. I willed my magic to spring forward, but I couldn't get it to cooperate. Couldn't get it to surface with enough power to do anything that might help.

Somewhere in the background, I heard someone call my name. Castiel. Castiel was calling my name. I hoped he at least killed the other angel. I hoped he would kill this one. Me dying wouldn't feel like such a waste, then. Castiel was just going to have to find someone else to get him his powers back.

It suddenly started to feel a bit easier. Maybe I was unconscious; I wasn't quite sure. There were slices of the road. Of the angel holding onto me. But there was mostly just... nothing. Until the world seemed to come back into focus again, slowly but surely.

I could still feel the angel's grip on my throat, but it wasn't as tight as before. After a moment, I could blink the world back into focus again. The angel didn't look at me. His eyes were fixed on something behind me. I opened my mouth and croaked out the ancient words. I gathered the strength to hold onto his hand around my throat, pushed the burning magic out through my own hands.

He didn't seem to notice his flesh burning at first. Too focused on whatever was going on. But when he *did* notice, he cried out in pain. As he let go of me, I fell to the ground. Coughing and sputtering as I clutched at my sore throat.

I heard a commotion off to my side, and when I looked over, Castiel had the angel in a death grip. The other one had already joined Cadriel on the ground, a wound staining his shirt red.

Dead.

"I won't expose you!" the angel begged, pleading with Castiel. "I will say you got killed. I'll get them off your back."

"*Lies.*"

Castiel slammed the angel to the ground, and I swore I heard something break. The angel cried out in pain, but just as Castiel raised his sword to strike, the angel managed to get up on his feet, scuttling a few feet away. The tip of Castiel's sword struck the ground where the angel had been just seconds before.

I got on my feet, my head feeling slightly better. I noticed the way one of his wings seemed a bit crooked.

Was that what had broken earlier? Then at least, he wouldn't be able to fly out of here. But he could still run. Not that I'd let him.

I cast my magic wide, tethering him to the place where he stood. The angel looked at me, a frantic sort of panic on his face. Castiel moved toward him slowly, and I caught a glimpse of the rage that was there. I shuddered. I wouldn't want to be on the receiving end of that anger.

"If you think you'll leave here unscathed...," he said, his voice barely audible. I knew the angel heard every word, though. "Then you're a fool."

"Castiel..."

Castiel pointed the sword at him. "Take my name out of your mouth. I know your face. Don't think I've forgotten."

"It was a long time ago, brother. I was..."

"You were one of the ones that did it, weren't you?" Castiel stood right in front of the angel, but I kept my distance. I had a feeling that Castiel had some things he needed to get off his chest.

"I was ordered to be there!" the angel cried. "You know I can't oppose a direct order."

"So, you killed her," Castiel stated.

"No, I swear!" The desperation in the angel's voice was clear. "I didn't kill your human. I was just..."

"There," Castiel filled in. "You were just there. And now you are here."

"Please..."

"You are here," Castiel continued as if he hadn't spoken. "And you *dare* lay your hand on her."

I froze. Was he talking about me? Must have been. "Castiel, end this before the rest come looking for them," I said, eager to get out of the open field.

"You're right," Castiel agreed. "This has gone on long enough."

The angel didn't even have time to scream before Castiel's sword pierced his abdomen. I flinched but forced myself to watch as he fell to the ground, as dead as the other two. Castiel tore his sword free, and the blood dripped from the steel. I sank down onto my knees, my body giving out. He was by my side in a matter of seconds.

"Danika." I felt his hands on me. I felt him stroking the hair out of my face. "Are you alright?"

"I don't know," I said. "I think so."

Castiel swore under his breath. "Damn them. If he had killed you..."

"Then you wouldn't get your wings back."

Castiel looked stunned for a moment. "No, that's not it."

I opened my mouth, only to close it again. What did he mean then? I looked over to the side, needing to step back for a second. "My blade. He threw it somewhere."

Castiel instantly got on his feet. "I'll find it; don't get up. Once you have it back, we'll try to find a place to stay for the night."

I breathed in, the sensation burning down my throat. "I'd kill for an actual bed tonight."

"Then we'll find a place with a bed." Castiel rummaged around for a while longer by the side of the road, then returned with my blade. "There. He hadn't thrown it far."

"Thank you." I took it and stood up, the sudden dizziness almost knocking me on my ass. I felt strong arms around me, and before I knew it, Castiel had lifted me into his arms. "What are you doing?"

"You're not walking," he said, searching around for something. When he spotted our bags thrown across the ground, he bent down and picked them up, like it was the easiest thing in the world.

"I am perfectly able to walk," I protested.

"You almost passed out just standing there," he pointed out. "Let me do this, and we'll get out of the open much quicker. The rest of them are still out here somewhere."

Well, he wasn't wrong. And now three more of their brothers were dead. I wondered if Cadriel was someone important. He certainly seemed to think so himself.

Holding onto Castiel's shoulder, I relaxed against him. Getting carried wasn't so bad. He was warm, and I realized that I felt safe there in his arms.

Imagine that.

CHAPTER 11

As it turned out, the town was a bit further away than we had initially thought. I could see it, but it was far off in the distance.

"Are you sure you wanna carry me?" I asked. "I feel okay; you don't have to."

Castiel gave me a look. "I told you, it's not a problem. And you're not okay. You were almost choked out back there. That can really damage your brain."

I grinned. "Are you saying I have brain damage?"

Castiel rolled his eyes. "No, but I'm still not convinced you're fine. I'll continue carrying you."

I sighed. "Alright, if you want to carry me this badly, then you can."

"It's not that I *want* to..."

"Oh, yes you do. I see how it is." I poked him in the chest. *Oh. Firm.* "You love being the big bad man, rescuing the helpless woman from the angels. Is that it?"

Castiel huffed out a short laugh. "Yeah, that's exactly it. I needed a boost to my masculinity."

"That's what I thought." I winked at him. "If you ever get tired of walking, I'll be sure to return the favor."

"I'll keep that in mind," he said, smirking. "Good thing I'm not twice your size or anything."

"I know." I chuckled. "You're just so dainty."

Castiel's laugh made his chest rumble. I couldn't help but laugh a little, too. It felt good after everything that had happened. After a while, Castiel stopped and looked up. I did also and thought I saw the distant outlines of a swarm of angels. They were so far up that they probably couldn't make us out, but knowing they were up there was enough to make me nervous. I didn't have the energy to fight if they were to descend from the sky.

"We should probably get off the road," Castiel said. "The trees will offer some protection."

"Yeah, you're probably right," I agreed and looked up one more time. I wanted to make sure they weren't getting any closer. "It's not very far to the town by the looks of it, better to be safe during the last bit of distance."

He nodded, stepped off the road, and back into the forest. It wasn't as thick as before, but it was better than nothing. I couldn't see the angels through the leaves of the trees, so hopefully, the angels couldn't see us either in case they decided to fly lower. Castiel needed to step around the rocks and the uneven ground now that we weren't on the road anymore, and I felt bad that I added to his burden.

"I can walk if it's too much."

"No more talk about you walking," Castiel retorted. "I don't mind."

Fine. I wasn't going to keep pushing. He'd set me down eventually. A thought struck me as I thought about the three angels that Castiel had killed. "What happens to angels when they die? It's not like they can go to Heaven."

Castiel smiled at my bad joke. "Not a lot of humans go there, either. My kind faces the same end as most others."

"Hell?" I asked, only half-joking. Castiel shook his head.

"No, not Hell. We return to the ground."

"So wormfood, basically."

"I guess that's one way of putting it."

"Doesn't that seem just a little..." I searched for the right word. "Anticlimactic? I mean, these are angels we're talking about. Aren't they supposed to be holy or something? Servants to God himself. And they just go into the ground when they die?"

"Humans are supposed to be made in God's image," Castiel said. "And they go into the ground when their lives end. Why should it be different for my kind?"

I shrugged. "I guess that's true. But I bet they don't like that, Gabriel and the other archangels."

"No, I don't imagine they do," Castiel said. "Meeting the same end as humans must feel humiliating for them."

"I don't really understand their hatred of humanity," I firmly stated. "Or of the Nephilim, for that matter. It hasn't always been this bad. My grandfather told me stories of what life was like before the angels came down to Earth."

Castiel sighed. "I'm not sure when it happened. The laws about fraternizing with the humans have been in place for centuries. But it wasn't until recently they've actually been enforced with such vigor. There is this obsession with purity that started to spring up. I don't know why. They started to see the humans as less than them. A lower standing being. I'm sure there were Nephilim wandering around the Earth before, too. But it's gotten so much worse for the younger ones ever since this purity obsession started. They say the Nephilim are tainting the bloodline."

"It doesn't make any sense, though," I said. "The Nephilim haven't done anything to taint the bloodline. The angels should be at fault, if anything."

His expression hardened, and I hurried to clarify what I meant. "I'm not saying it's wrong for an angel and human to be together; you know I don't think so. But with Heaven's logic, the angel should be the one to blame. Not the Nephilim."

He nodded. "Some *do* pay. Even if there is no offspring."

I looked at him, hating the pain that settled in the furrow of his brow. "I know, Castiel. And that's not right. It's not right at all."

There were some lights shining through the trees, and soon, the forest ended completely. We finally reached the town, and I started to feel a little more at ease. Surely, there would be somewhere for us to sleep. Somewhere for us to regain our strength. The houses were small, with just the occasional tall building here and there. The only light source were the streetlights peppered along the cobbled streets. It almost looked like something from another time, apart from the occasional heli parked over to the sides.

"I really do think I can walk now," I said. I *did* feel a lot better. I guess I just needed a moment to gather myself after everything, and my throat barely hurt anymore. Castiel carefully set me down, his arm ready to catch me if I should lose my balance. It was kind of sweet, actually.

"Do you think there's a hotel or something around here?" Castiel asked. "Maybe it's too small a town."

"Maybe," I said. "Let's have a look around. If there

isn't one, we'll just try and find an empty shed or something."

He scoffed. "I thought you wanted a bed."

I did. I really, really did. "Fingers crossed for a hotel then."

It didn't take very long to explore the few streets that made up the central part of town. I counted one café, one clothing store, and one general market. A bit further down the street were two hair salons on opposite sides. That was just about everything this town had to offer.

But to my surprise, we managed to find a small motel. It was a tiny place, one of the skinniest buildings I had ever seen. It had maybe three or four stories, so there wasn't much going on there. I didn't understand how they managed to stay in business with such a small establishment. But at least it was there, and that was enough for me.

A small woman in her late twenties sat behind the front desk, reading something on her electronic reader. Her auburn hair had been piled high on top of her head, and she wore thick rimmed glasses. When we walked through the door, her eyes went wide behind those frames.

I then realized how we must look. Castiel's clothes had blood on them, and I probably looked like a mess. I tried to straighten my clothes and brush the dirt off my pants. It didn't really do much to improve the way I looked, though, so I decided to just put on a big smile as I walked up to the woman.

"Hello," I said, hoping we hadn't scared her too bad already. "My friend and I would like two rooms for the night. Do you have any available?"

Her mouth hung open for a moment, and then she gathered herself together long enough to look at the screen in front of her. "There is one room on the top floor available. I'm afraid it's our most expensive one."

"We need two rooms," I spat back. "Are you sure there isn't another one?"

She shook her head. "There's a school event this week. We're pretty much fully booked."

I sighed. "Are there any other hotels in town?"

She shook her head. Of course not. That was a silly question. "It's fine," Castiel jumped in. "We'll take the room."

I glared at him. Sure, we had shared a couch when we needed to back at the cabin in the woods. But this was a hotel. How did he not also want his privacy?

"Are you sure?" I asked.

Castiel nodded. "It's only for one night."

I reached for my bag to get the credits out, but he beat me to it. He slammed a pile of credits on the counter and looked at the woman. "Will this be enough?" he asked.

The woman nodded. "Yes, sir. Will it just be for the one night?"

"It will," Castiel said with a nod.

We were given a keycard and took the elevator up to the third floor. There was hardly any use of an elevator in such a small place, but I was glad I didn't have to climb the stairs. I was exhausted after a whole day of walking, not to mention what had happened just a short while ago.

Should we have gotten rid of the bodies? Maybe not. It would've taken too long, and the other angels already knew where their brothers had been. They'd find the spot regardless if we'd gotten rid of the bodies or not. I didn't like that we were still so close to the road where we'd been attacked. But at the same time, we needed to rest.

Castiel opened the door to the room, and we stepped inside. It wasn't very big, despite the girl saying that it was one of their more expensive rooms. A large bed took up most of the space, and there was a closet to the right of the door. A small window was perched on one side of the wall, and a large screen was hanging on the other side of the bed.

"I guess this will have to do." I sighed and slung my bag onto the floor. My whole body felt like it was made of lead, my limbs heavy and aching.

Castiel nodded toward the bathroom. "The shower is yours if you want it. I'll shower after you."

I nodded and rummaged through my bag for some clean clothes. A shower would do me good. I felt gross after several days on the move.

The water pressure was pretty bad, but at least the water was warm. I scrubbed my skin until I was red and raw, letting the dirt and grime wash off of me. Castiel stood right outside the door when I was done, a towel in one hand. We passed each other without saying a word.

And as he showered, I combed my hair and put it in a braid to get it out of my face. I crawled into bed, loving the feel of the soft mattress and fluffy comforter.

The water then stopped running in the shower, and just a few moments later, Castiel walked out, a towel slung around his hips.

Suddenly, I wasn't so tired anymore.

CHAPTER 12

Why did he have to walk around like that? So... naked. He must think it's funny, seeing me get all flustered.

"Didn't you bring a fresh set of clothes?" I asked.

Castiel looked at me, his face less severe than before. And then he looked down at himself and smiled.

"Why?" he asked. "Is there something wrong with how I'm dressed now?"

"You're *not* dressed now," I pointed out.

"I'll put something on if this makes you uncomfortable."

I didn't know why, but it felt ridiculous to ask him to put on a shirt. Like I was some child who had never seen a man before. Hell, I had seen *him* several times already.

"Do whatever you want," I mumbled. "I'm going to sleep." I lied down, turning my back to him. I could hear him going through his bag. I also heard the towel drop to the floor, and I clutched the comforter tighter in my hands. Was he naked? I glanced over my shoulder; of course, I did.

Not naked, thank goodness, but dressed in a pair of sweatpants. He saw me looking and gestured toward the bed.

"Are you okay with sharing again?"

"I nodded. "Of course. There's no sense in me having this whole bed to myself."

I felt him climb on, and then under the covers. We weren't touching, but I could feel the heat from his body despite the distance between us. I didn't think he was asleep; his breathing wasn't deep enough for that.

I turned, looking at him. Castiel was sitting, his back propped up against the headboard. When he saw me turn, he looked down at me.

"Can't sleep?"

I sat up, shaking my head. "No. I was exhausted a moment ago, but now I can't seem to relax. How about you?"

He shook his head. "No, I can't seem to relax, either."

"Were you hurt before? Did any of the angels get you?"

Castiel smiled. "No, I'm fine."

Physically, at least. I thought back to everything that had been said, and the rage and hurt I had seen displayed on his face. "Can I ask you about her?" I asked quietly. "About Sydney?"

He stiffened, and for a moment, I feared that I'd made him angry. But then he just hung his head for a moment before he turned to me with a nod. "What do you want to know?"

I wasn't sure. I had a million questions floating around in my head. "What was she like?"

"She was kind, much like yourself. But quieter and more tame." He shook his head, a fond smile on his lips. "And she was funny. Beautiful."

"You loved her."

"I did. For a while, she was my world." He sighed. "We were both very young. Well, I suppose that's debatable as far as my age goes. But in the grand scheme of things, we were both very young. Foolish."

"How did the angels find out?"

"Oh, they always find out somehow. And I wasn't very careful." He swallowed.

"You blame yourself. For her death."

Castiel looked at me. "Of course. If it weren't for me..."

"It's not you who made up these senseless laws," I

interrupted. "To love..." I shook my head. "It can't be wrong. And no one should be killed for it."

He stared. Actually stared. "You really believe that, don't you?"

I frowned. "Of course."

"Not many people share your sentiment," he said to me. "But thank you for saying it."

I shrugged. "Shouldn't be such a controversial opinion," I replied. "Despite what I think of your kind, I'm starting to learn that not everyone is as bad as others."

Castiel took my hand over the covers, and he squeezed it before letting go. "Thank you."

For some reason, my cheeks burned. "Let's get some sleep." I pulled away and lied back down. Castiel did as well, but he didn't close his eyes.

"Have you made up your mind about getting me my wings back?"

I hadn't. After what happened earlier, I had no doubt in my mind that Castiel would never do Heaven's bidding again. There would be no harm in restoring him to his former self because he wouldn't be like them. He *wasn't* like them.

"I'll do it."

The words left my mouth before I knew what I was saying. I hadn't been sure, but I thought I was making the right choice. Right then and there, it felt like the right thing to do. He turned his head and looked at me.

"You will?"

"I will. As soon as we find someplace safe. I'm still not sure if I can do it, though."

"I think you can," he whispered quietly. He shifted to his side and propped his head up on his hand. "I really am thankful, Danika."

"Yeah, well..." I didn't know what to say. He was just so... happy about it. "Happy to help."

Castiel smiled. "Can I ask you something?"

"Sure."

"Did you always have your powers?"

I shook my head. "No, they started coming in after my parents died."

"I've heard that the magic can be triggered when something traumatic happens," Castiel said. "What was it like?"

"Unexpected," I responded with a little laugh. "No one in my family had powers, so I suppose the gene was dormant somewhere in the bloodline."

"It's not unheard of. That a witch is unaware of the powers within her before they are awakened."

"I guess not," I mumbled. "Most of the witches I know come from long lines of magical families. I think it was just hard to start thinking of myself as something other than human."

"It *is* hard," he agreed. "To have to accept that you are something other than what you used to be."

"Was it like that for you?" I asked. "When you fell?"

"Of course. I had to learn how to be human without all the things I had taken for granted before."

He smiled. "Do you know how slow walking is when you're used to flying through the sky?"

I huffed out a laugh. "Yeah, I imagine it must be very slow."

There was a moment's silence where we just looked at each other. It struck me that it didn't feel awkward. At all.

"How old were you?" Castiel asked. "When your parents died."

"Nine," I answered. "I don't really remember much about them. Bits and pieces, although I'm not sure how much of it is real and how much I've made up over the years."

"That's very young to lose your family," Castiel said and reached out to touch my hand again.

"I didn't lose all of my family. My grandfather took me in. I was lucky."

"Not many would agree."

I smiled. "Maybe not. But I never felt neglected or forgotten. He was always good to me."

"And then you got your magic."

"I did." I remembered that first time when I felt the electric static of my powers rushing through me. I didn't understand what was happening, but when I accidentally burned my grandfather with my bare hand, he quickly figured out what was going on.

"How did an orphan with no history of magic in her family come to be the leader of a coven?" Castiel asked. "I must say, it's impressive."

I smiled. "My coven doesn't work as many others

do. I didn't take my position by forcing out the former leader. It was given to me. My sisters gave it to me. And I'm a leader only in name. We all carry that coven on our shoulders."

Castiel nodded thoughtfully. "I see. Well, I'm more and more certain that I made the right choice to come to you then. If you are held in such high regard with your sisters, then you must be truly special."

My throat closed. I didn't know what to say. I really hoped Tatia and the others were okay. I hoped I would see them again soon.

Castiel still held my hand.

I only just realized that. It felt nice. My heart skipped a beat when he flipped my hand around and ran his thumb over my palm.

"What are you doing?" I asked, voice low. Castiel swallowed.

"I'm not sure."

I slowly pulled my hand away. "Maybe we should discuss what to do tomorrow."

Castiel cleared his throat and nodded. "Yes. Good idea. I, um... we should probably leave first thing, and we'll grab some food along the way. And if you're not too tired, we should probably get to a city. There's one not far from here. We can find another heli there."

"Something less noisy than the abomination you were driving around in, I hope."

Some of the tension left his shoulders at my words. "Yes. Something less noisy."

"But how do we know the angels are gone?" I asked. "We'll need to be careful."

"Of course." Castiel paused, and for a moment, it looked like he might say something. But he just lied down on his back, looking up at the ceiling. "Go to sleep. We'll make sure the angels are gone tomorrow. If they are, we'll get ourselves to the city as fast as we can."

I nodded. "Okay."

I really hoped the angels would've passed through. That they hadn't continued their search for us. But I knew that was foolish of me to think. We just killed more of their brothers, and I suspected that they thought I still needed to be punished for what I had done for the Nephilim over the years.

Castiel's breathing started to deepen by my side. I looked over at him; he was beautiful, even in sleep. There was no going around that. He looked calm. Peaceful. I started to relax a little. If someone had told me just a few days ago that I would be lying in bed with an angel, a fallen one at that, then I would've thought them crazy.

Yet, here I was. Here *he* was. I hadn't talked about my parents in years, but it felt good to share that part of my life with him. It wasn't something I thought of very often.

I closed my eyes, trying to fall asleep, and after a while, my body started to feel heavier and heavier. My mind started to drift. I turned my back to Castiel, and just as I was about to fall asleep, I felt a strong arm wrap around my waist. I glanced over my shoulder at him. He was so close and pulled me closer still.

I thought he was still asleep—it looked like he was, at least. I considered waking him, but it felt good being held like that. I couldn't remember the last time I was. I felt his warm breath against my neck, a strong hand on my belly, and I started to drift off to sleep.

We were both startled awake when a knock sounded at the door.

CHAPTER 13

Castiel flung his arm away from me, and for a confused moment, we just looked at each other.

"Did I...?" He cleared his throat. "I mean, I'm sorry. I didn't realize..."

Another knock at the door brought us back to reality. "Get your sword," I said and got out of bed. Castiel did as I said, and I grabbed my own weapon from my jacket before I went over to the door.

"Are you really going to open it?" Castiel asked.

"If it were the angels, don't you think they

would've barged in here without knocking? It's probably the receptionist or something." Still, I held my blade firm.

I unlocked the door, opening it just a few inches. The hallway outside was dark, but there was a tall man standing out there. For a moment, I thought it really *was* one of the angels. He even had a sword strapped to his hip. Before thinking, I charged at him with my blade.

"Hey!" he called out and jumped out of the way. "There's no need for that."

I stilled. "Micah?"

Castiel was right behind me, and his eyes narrowed when he saw Micah. "What are you doing here?"

"Interrupting something, clearly." Micah walked through the door, a wide grin on his face when he took in our rumpled appearance.

"Really, though," I said and crossed my arms over my chest. "How did you find us?"

"I just followed the trail of dead angels. It wasn't very hard." He turned a bit more serious when he saw our displeased faces. "I followed you after you left. It's like I said yesterday, you aren't as quiet as you seem to think."

"The dead angels are still on the road?" I asked.

"I passed the spot just a short while ago," Micah said. "They were still there."

I looked at Castiel. Their brothers hadn't come to claim the bodies. Why not?

"But why come after us?" Castiel asked, putting his

sword back against the wall. "You had been in hiding for months. Why go out now?"

Micah shrugged. "I like you guys. Would you believe me if I said that I simply missed you?"

"No."

A low chuckle escaped him. "Alright, then. The truth is, there were some angels snooping around the cabin right after you left. I got out without them noticing me, but just barely. I figured I'd come after you. Safety in numbers and all."

"So, they knew we were at the cabin."

Micah shrugged. "I guess so. I didn't stick around to find out what they wanted."

"But how did you track us?" Castiel asked, a hard expression on his face.

"Let's just say it's clear that you two are used to living in the city. You also didn't cover your tracks. It wasn't very hard."

I hadn't even considered hiding our tracks as we walked through the forest, and Castiel clearly hadn't either. "So, now what?" I asked. "You're just going to tag along with us?"

"If you don't mind."

"We mind," Castiel said at once. Micah's jaw tensed.

"You won't get far without a place to hide out in," he said. "I can provide such a place. All I'm asking is that you take me with you."

I looked at Castiel. We *did* need a place to hide out, a place where I could restore his powers. And

Micah *had* managed to hide for months out in the cabin. Maybe it wasn't such a bad idea to take him up on his offer.

"I think we should do it," I mumbled to the angel.

"Absolutely not," Castiel protested. "They're looking for him, too. We'll have even more angels on our butts if we go with him."

"Castiel," I said calmly. "We need a safe place. Otherwise, I won't be able to..." I glanced at Micah. He didn't need to know what Castiel wanted my help with. "I won't be able to do what we discussed last night."

He looked at me. "We said we'd go to the next city over.

"To find a safe place, yes. Micah has such a place. It will save us time if we just go with him."

I could still see some resistance in his eyes, but then he just shrugged. "Fine. We will go with you to your safe spot. But after that, we part ways. Understood?"

Micah nodded. "Understood. Best to get going, don't you think? It's early in the morning; there aren't very many people outside."

We both nodded and started gathering our things. I hated the idea that we were going to have to do *more* walking already, but it was probably best to get out of town with the angels so close by. The front desk was empty when we got downstairs, so I just left the keycard there. Castiel was the first to look outside, one hand on the hilt of his sword.

"I think we can go," he said.

We followed him outside. I pulled the hood of my jacket over my head despite it being nice and warm outside. Micah gestured for us to follow him, and I could tell Castiel was hesitant. But I grabbed his hand and dragged him along, and to my surprise, there was no resistance.

After a few minutes, we stopped in front of a heli. Micah smiled wide.

"Isn't she a beauty?"

"This is yours?" I asked, taking in the machinery. It was one of the newer models, state of the art technology. I had only seen this model in videos, never in real life. Not even in the nicer parts of my hometown.

"It is now!" Micah exclaimed, beaming as he laid a hand on the exterior.

"So, you stole it."

We both turned to look at Castiel, who stood a few steps back with a look of disapproval on his face.

"I'm borrowing it," Micah said. "This way, we'll be out of here in no time."

I chewed on my bottom lip. I didn't love the fact that he had stolen it, but at the same time, it would be nice to get to the safe spot as quickly as possible.

"Maybe the owner won't miss it," I said, and Castiel crinkled his forehead at me.

"You don't think they'll miss this brand new heli? It must've cost hundreds of thousands of credits."

"I know, but..."

"Maybe we can have this discussion in the air?"

Micah asked and unlocked the aircraft. He hopped into the driver's seat, starting the engine. It purred to life, barely making a sound. A far cry from Castiel's old vehicle.

"I don't know about this," Castiel said, shaking his head.

"Well, you'll have to decide quickly," Micah told him.

"And why is that?"

The Nephila glanced skyward. "We have company."

Both Castiel and I whirled around, necks craned to see the sky. Micah was right. The angels were out, despite the morning light. Castiel swore under his breath, then he turned to me and hoisted me up into the heli. He pulled himself up, and before he could even close the door, we were in the air.

"Do you think they saw us?" I asked.

"I'd say so," Micah said and veered left. "Why else would they be out so early?"

That's what I had thought, too. Micah steered the heli through the small streets of town, keeping the vehicle low for the time being. Castiel and I had our eyes glued to the swarm above us; it was impossible to look away. I didn't see Gabriel amongst them, but there were still at least fifteen of them flying up there. No doubt they were there on his orders.

"This safe spot of yours," I said. "Will we uncover it if they follow us?"

"No, I don't think so," Micah answered. "But I

don't like the thought of them following us there anyway." We need to get them off our trail somehow."

Castiel turned to me. "Is there something you can do? Can you hide us? At least long enough to confuse them?"

I nodded. "I can try. But I think we need to put some distance between us and them. Hiding an aircraft like this will take a lot of effort. I don't know if I can keep it up for long."

"Then let's get going," Micah jumped in and steered the heli up.

We rose rapidly, and soon, we were just ahead of the angels. I looked through the rear window and saw the triumph on their faces. They thought they had us. I really, really hoped they were wrong.

I tried to breathe, tried to center myself to be able to put as much of my powers as possible into hiding us. When one of them flew up alongside the aircraft and jerked on the door, I jumped in my seat. Castiel placed his hand on my leg, and our eyes met for a second. I calmed down a little at his touch. Things would be alright. We just needed to get away.

"Doesn't this thing go any faster?" I asked. Micah nodded.

"I can probably get it to the next level. I've actually never tried."

I leaned back against my seat, closing my eyes for a second. "Lovely."

"Hey," Castiel whispered. "You've got this. They can't get to us in here."

I knew that was a lie, and I could see that he also didn't believe his own words. But I smiled and grabbed his hand. "I know." It felt good to hold onto him as he centered me in the moment. Micah flipped a switch, and then the heli took off. The angels were right behind us, but the distance grew bit by bit.

"I'm going to make a sharp turn once we reach those cliffs over there," Micah said. "When I do, I need you to do your thing, Danika."

I swallowed. "Okay."

The cliffs in question weren't very big, but it might be enough to make it seem like we've gone in a different direction. If I could hide us long enough to get the angels confused, that is. They approached rapidly, and I took another deep breath. This was it. Micah was gripping the steering levers tightly, and I could tell that he was just waiting for the exact moment to turn. I stole one more look behind us. The angels weren't right behind us, but they were gaining speed.

"Okay, Danika!" Micah called out. "Go!"

I was smooshed against Castiel's side as Micah took the sharp turn, and Castiel put an arm around me to keep me in place. I started speaking the ancient words, closing my eyes to focus. I pulled on my magic, made it flow through me, outside of me. When I opened my eyes again, I saw a light sheen that covered the aircraft. It was working! I kept speaking, kept pushing my powers out.

"Shut down the engine!" Castiel commanded, and I saw Micah push a button that made the heli quiet down. We slowed, eventually just hanging in mid-air. A solid, invisible lump of metal and glass. If the angels flew into the aircraft, we'd be discovered.

I looked outside, still speaking the words. They were there, but they didn't look right at us. Instead, they searched the area with confusion in their eyes. A smile spread on Castiel's face, something like pride in his expression. They passed right by us, flying slowly while they looked around.

One of them was right outside the window to my side. If the window had been open, I could've reached out and touched him. This could uncover us. If he just moved a few feet to his left, he would bump into the aircraft.

I grabbed hold of the seat underneath my body, needing to hold onto something to keep my hands from shaking. Sweat was running down my face, and every now and then, my voice cracked.

Why were they still here? Why hadn't they moved on if they couldn't see us? I wasn't going to be able to keep the spell up for much longer. I saw Castiel looking at me out of the corner of my eye, but I couldn't focus on him. I just had to keep it up for a few more minutes. Surely, they would go away soon.

I saw one of them gesture the others to follow him, and then the whole swarm took off. They looked like they were headed east, and I hoped they thought we'd taken off in that direction.

"Danika, let go," Castiel said. I shook my head, not wanting us out in the open quite yet. They could still return. He cupped my face, forcing me to meet his eyes. "Let go. You're pale as a ghost."

"We better get moving," Micah said and started the engine. "I'll keep us low in the sky for a while, but I think we're in the clear."

I stared into Castiel's gaze, barely hearing the Nephila. Castiel nodded, stroking a thumb over my cheek. "Let go."

Slowly but surely, I released my hold of the magic. The sheen that covered us disappeared, and we were once again visible. Micah sped up the aircraft, steering west. Castiel still held my face in his big hand.

"Are you okay?" he asked, voice low. I nodded, but my hands were still shaking, and I was breathing heavily.

"If she passes out, the seat next to mine reclines," Micah called out over his shoulder. Castiel gave him a murderous look.

"She's fine. I've got her."

"Sure you do, big guy."

I slumped against Castiel's side, and his arm around my shoulders tightened. I was just too tired to sit upright. "Sorry," I said. "That took more out of me than I had expected."

"Don't apologize," he said. "Rest. I've got you."

CHAPTER 14

I must've fallen asleep because when I opened my eyes, we were flying into a city. The tall buildings and flashing lights reminded me of the nicer parts of my hometown. This place didn't seem quite as run-down as some parts of my own city were.

Micah flew us to a place at the very edge of the city and parked outside a massive, expensive-looking building.

"This is where we're hiding out?" Castiel asked. Micah shook his head.

"I'm just leaving the heli here. Should blend in with all the others. We walk the last bit."

It was smart to leave the vehicle somewhere else, just in case there were angels around. Castiel helped me down from the aircraft, and when we were both on solid ground, he still held onto my hand. Micah gave us one look and smirked. At least he didn't say anything. If he had, I think Castiel would've killed him on the spot.

We walked through the streets, lined with one fancy house after another. Micah turned onto a side street, and the buildings instantly started to look less expensive. We were obviously out of the rich neighborhood.

Stopping outside a yellow townhouse, the paint faded from the sun, Micah knocked three times on the front door. It took a moment, but then a woman in her early fifties cracked open the door a few inches. Her brown eyes flitted between us, seemingly confused. Then she looked closer at Micah and flung the door open.

"Micah!" she shrieked and pulled him in for a massive hug. "Oh, it's you. It's really you."

"Keep your voice down, mother," Micah said, smiling wide. "Can we do this inside?"

"Oh, of course, of course." She let go of him and eyed the two strangers beside him. Her eyes grew a bit weary when she looked at Castiel, obviously recognizing the angelic features. "Who are your friends?"

"Just some people I picked up on the way," Micah

said and walked inside. "I was hoping they could stay here for a few days."

"If you think it's wise," his mother said, but it was clear that she wasn't the biggest fan of the idea.

"We'll be out of your hair in no time," I assured her. "But we'll be very grateful if we can stay for just a little while."

Her face softened a little. "Come on in."

We walked inside, into the warm home where Micah must've grown up. The walls were covered with paintings, real ones. I wondered if the woman was an artist. I spotted several pieces depicting what could only be Micah as a boy, dressed with the same shit-eating grin he wore as a grown man.

"These are beautiful," I said, and Micah's mother smiled.

"Thank you, dear. Just something I do to pass the time."

Micah scoffed. "She's being humble. She used to paint for the mayor of this town. He was one of her biggest patrons."

She blushed and swatted at her son. "Yes, I suppose I have sold a piece or two back in my day. But let's not dwell in the hallway. Come in, please."

She led us to a small but beautiful living room. The walls were just as covered in here, beautiful landscapes and depictions of skyscrapers and buildings.

"Have a seat," she said and gestured at the couch. "I'll make us all something to eat. You must be hungry!" She looked at her son. "Micah, will you help me?"

I smiled as he trotted along next to his mother. It was so obvious that she was about to get every bit of information she could about us. I sat down, and Castiel did the same. He looked a little out of place in here. I wasn't sure why. He just seemed to dominate the small room.

"This is nice," I said. "We can probably rest here for a few days, and then we'll go somewhere remote, just you and me. I'll restore you then."

He nodded, but his mind seemed far away. "Sounds good."

"Did you hear a word I said?" I asked him, and Castiel turned to look at me. I could practically see the wheels turning in his head. "What is it?"

"She doesn't like that I'm here," he explained and nodded in the direction of the kitchen.

"You *do* look kind of intimidating," I pointed out. "Especially with that massive sword strapped to your hip."

He glanced down as if he hadn't considered the sword. "I guess. I'm just thinking that she might not have had the best experience with my kind. There's something in her eyes..."

"Micah's father was an angel," I said. "She can't be totally opposed to you guys."

Castiel shook his head. "Micah doesn't know who sired him. That's usually a sign that things didn't happen... voluntarily."

Realization dawned on me. "You mean she got pregnant after being forced to—"

"Maybe." He shook his head. "I don't want to assume, but I didn't like the look on her face when she saw me."

"Maybe she was just scared for Micah's sake. I'm sure having a Nephila child would be cause for concern with the angels going after them."

"Yeah," he said. "Let's hope you're right."

Our conversation was cut short when the others returned, Micah with a large tray of food in his hands. He placed it on the small table in front of them, and his mother clapped her hands together.

"There we are! Help yourselves to as much as you'd like. There's plenty more where that came from!"

"Thank you," I said and grabbed a sandwich. "You are so kind to let us into your home."

"Oh, don't mention it, dear. Any friend of Micah's is a friend of mine." Her eyes lingered on Castiel as she spoke the words, still unsure about him. "Micah tells me you're in a bit of trouble."

"You could say that," I said, biting down on the soft bread.

Micah's mother looked a little uncomfortable for a moment. She turned her eyes to Castiel and opened her mouth, only to close it again. He looked right at her, smiling.

"If you have a question for me, feel free to ask," he said.

She swallowed and turned crimson red, but she sat up straight and looked him right in the eye.

"Will it be dangerous to have you here?" she asked. "For my son? For me and for this young lady?"

Castiel hesitated. "It might be. If you don't want me here, I'm happy to leave."

I put one hand on his knee. "Castiel, no."

"Mother, there is no greater danger in having him here than it is to have me or Danika here." Micah's eyes turned to me. "She is a witch."

His mother's eyes widened. "Are you really?"

I nodded. "I am." Micah spoke again.

"She helps my kind, the ones who don't want to be what we are."

Something flashed across the woman's face. "Could she help you?"

"She could. But you know how I feel about that."

She sighed. "I wish you would reconsider. It'd make life so much easier for you, my boy."

"Maybe so," he said and squeezed her hand. "But I've never been one to take the easy way out."

His mother shook her head. "No, I suppose you haven't." Her gaze returned to Castiel again." If my son is alright with having you here, then I am, too. As long as you live under my roof, you will be safe."

Castiel bowed his head to her. "Thank you."

"May I ask how?" I asked."How is this place safe?"

Micah turned to look at his mother. "She struck a deal with a witch a long time ago. This house does not exist."

I looked around, trying to sense the magic that kept the house hidden. I couldn't feel it. But if he said it was true, then I suppose I must believe him.

We ate our meal quietly, listening to Micah and his mother as they talked. It was pleasant to see the love so clearly in her eyes as she looked at her son. I didn't know my mother, and for the first time in my adult life, I regretted that. Once the tray was empty, Micah's mother turned to her son.

"Why don't you show Danika the garden? I have some herbs that might interest her."

"That would be lovely," I said and stood up. "Thank you."

Both Micah and Castiel stood, too, and the older woman's gaze turned to Castiel. "Actually, if you wouldn't mind staying inside, I have something I'd like to speak with you about."

A flash of surprise came over him, but Castiel soon schooled his expression into neutrality. "Of course." He then turned to me. "Keep close to the house, okay?"

"It's not a very big garden," Micah said before I could answer. "You'll be able to see her at all times, big guy."

Castiel's eyes narrowed, but he didn't say anything. Micah offered his arm to me and led me to the back door. I looked over my shoulder, finding Castiel looking right at us. I smiled at him, and his face softened a little. Was he jealous? No, that was ridiculous. He was just looking out for me. He needed me to get what he wanted.

The fresh air was a nice change, and I breathed in deeply. Micah smiled and led me to a small patch of land where herbs of every variety grew.

"She likes to dabble with healing herbs," he said. "My mother doesn't get out much, so she tries to be as self-sufficient as possible."

"Smart woman," I responded and let go of his arm. I stooped in front of the herb garden and reached out to touch some of the leaves. "She has a good variety here," I said. "I'd be happy to teach her some tinctures that might be useful."

His face brightened. "She'd love that."

I glanced toward the house. Micah's mother and Castiel sat next to each other on the couch, serious expressions on their faces. "Do you know what she wanted to talk to him about?"

Micah's smiling face turned sour. "My father, I suppose. I think she wants to ask if Castiel knew him."

Flashes of mine and Castiel's earlier conversation popped into my mind. "You never knew him?"

"No," Micah said. "I don't think I would've liked to. She doesn't like to talk about him, but I have a feeling he wasn't a very good guy."

"And yet she wonders about him."

He nodded. "He has etched himself into her mind, and she can't let go. I think she hates him, but at the same time, she wants to know where he is now. I know she's curious about him."

"Aren't you?"

He shook his head. "I don't need him. I have her."

"You're very lucky," I said and placed a hand on his arm. "She seems like a wonderful mother."

He smiled again. "She is." Then his eyes flickered to the house, and he grinned even wider. I turned to look and saw Castiel staring right at us. At my hand on Micah's arm. I rolled my eyes. Definitely jealous. But why?

"I don't think he likes me very much," Micah said, raising a hand to wave at Castiel.

"He has no problem with the Nephilim," I said, and Micah shook his head.

"No, I don't think he does. I think it's more an issue of me pissing on his territory."

I raised an eyebrow. "His territory? I'd choose my next words carefully if I were you."

He chuckled. "You know what I mean. He doesn't like that I flirt with you."

"It's not like that between us," I said, but when I looked at Castiel, at the way he looked back at us, the words rang false. "He needs me for something."

Micah wiggled his eyebrows. "Yeah, he does."

I shoved his shoulder. "Not *that*. I'm helping him with something, that's all."

"Right." He winked at me. "Keep telling yourself that, sweetheart."

CHAPTER 15

Micah's mother took her son over to the side as we walked back into the house, eager to catch up after months of being apart. Castiel stood in the middle of the living room, and I suddenly didn't know where to look.

"Vera said we could have the two bedrooms upstairs," he said after a moment's silence.

"Vera?"

"Micah's mother."

Right. Of course. "Great!" I cheered. "I'll go bring my bag up."

Without saying anything, Castiel simply took both our bags and started heading upstairs. I stood there for a moment, looking at him. Then I shook my head and followed. It seemed like my bag-carrying days were over.

The next floor up was simply decorated, but neat and put together. Castiel handed me my bag and pointed to one of the rooms. "You'll be in there. I'm just next door."

"Okay," I said. "Are you sure you can sleep without me?"

It was a joke, but Castiel didn't laugh. Instead, his entire face turned pink. "I'll manage."

What the *fuck* was going on? First the staring, now this?

I had just opened the door to a small guest room when Castiel cleared his throat. I turned around and looked at him.

"You okay?"

He nodded. "Um... did you find any interesting herbs?"

I shrugged. "There was a little bit of everything. Why?"

"You just looked... happy."

"Shouldn't I look happy?"

He stepped closer. "I just mean that if you'd prefer staying here... Staying with Micah..."

I held up a hand to stop him. "Hold on. Who said anything about staying here with Micah?"

"You like him."

"He's nice. Very likable."

"And he likes you."

I frowned at him. "Castiel, what is this? I promised to help you. Why would you think I'd back out from that?"

He nodded slowly. I suddenly realized just how close he was standing. I could easily reach out a hand and touch him. Except he touched me first.

With my back pressed against the wall, Castiel cupped my face. He leaned down, close enough so that our noses were touching, and he clamped his eyes shut. My heart was going crazy in my chest, and I was too stunned to move. Softly, he stroked his thumb over my cheek, his lips a fraction from mine. I didn't move. Didn't know what to do. What I *wanted* to do.

"Danika..."

He said my name like a caress. Like it was precious. I finally broke free from my temporary paralysis and touched his chest. Ran my hands up the muscled surface, and a shiver ran down my back at the feel of him. So strong. So warm and beautiful. Castiel opened his eyes again, and I saw the hesitation there. He was conflicted. I couldn't blame him. I thought of her, too.

Sydney.

The woman he loved, whom I'd never met. And yet, I thought of her. Was that what he was worried about? Did he feel like he was betraying her by standing here with me?

"Castiel, it's okay," I whispered. I placed one hand

on the back of his neck and ran my fingers through his short hair. "It's okay."

I wasn't sure what I meant. If I wanted him to know that it was okay for him to kiss me, or if it was okay if he didn't.

I really hoped he would. I wanted to know what those full lips felt like against my own. I wanted to know what he tasted like.

"Oh, shit."

Micah's voice made us jump apart. I could feel my face turn red, and Castiel looked like he had just been caught stealing. The Nephila, however, looked like Christmas had come early.

"Don't let me interrupt," he said, laughter in his voice. "I was just getting some things from my old room."

He walked past us and went into the room where Castiel was going to be sleeping. So, Micah was giving up his room for the angel. What a good man. Micah soon emerged again, a pillow and a blanket in his arms.

"I hope you'll sleep well tonight." He nodded at us. "Or if you don't, please try to be quiet. My mother is a light sleeper." He winked as he passed me, and I turned even redder. Castiel looked like he was about to strangle Micah, but he just clenched his jaw and stayed quiet. The tension was thick enough to cut with a knife when Micah went back downstairs. I glanced over at Castiel, who didn't meet my eyes.

"I'm sorry," he said. "I shouldn't have..."

Oh. "It's okay."

"Maybe it would be best if we left first thing tomorrow," he said. "We'll find a place for you to get me back to how I'm supposed to be, and then you'll be free of me."

I didn't know what to say. "Is that what you want?"

He gave me a curt nod. "Yes. It's for the best. I won't be your problem for much longer."

Before I could say anything, he went into Micah's bedroom and closed the door. I stood there for a moment, stunned. He had almost kissed me. If Micah hadn't come upstairs, Castiel *definitely* would've kissed me. I looked at the closed door. Did he regret it? Had it just been a temporary lapse in judgment?

I didn't think so. Over the past few days, we had been growing closer. There had been that moment at the hotel, when he held my hand. I almost thought something might happen then. Maybe it would've if I hadn't pulled back. I put a finger to my mouth and touched it lightly. I could almost feel the shadow of him there. Almost.

Despite it not being very late, I decided to go to bed. The mattress was old, but I couldn't complain. It was still soft and comfortable, and the blanket I pulled up to my chin looked homemade. Micah's comment about his mother wanting to be self-sufficient ran through my mind. It wouldn't surprise me if she had also made the blanket. Maybe even some of her own clothes.

I didn't know anyone who created things like she did. Especially not among the witches, who could easily summon their desires with one simple spell. It was admirable for her to only rely on herself. Admirable, but perhaps a bit lonely.

As the sun started to set, I started thinking about my sisters back home. I should try and get to a phone soon, just to check in. I hoped they hadn't been bothered by any more angels. And I hoped Tatia could manage everything.

When this is all over, I'm going straight home to see them.

I bolted up into a sitting position when a knock at my door startled me. My heart started racing when Castiel came inside.

"May I come in?" he asked, something like nervousness in his deep voice. I nodded.

"Is everything alright?" I asked.

"Yeah. I just... I couldn't sleep."

"Why not?" I asked, even though I suspected I knew the answer. Castiel stood right in front of me, towering over me where I sat on the bed. He might've looked terrifying to anyone else. Big and strong, with that intense gaze fully focused on me.

But I wasn't afraid.

"I can't stop thinking about you," he muttered, almost whispering the words. My skin broke out into goosebumps. Castiel crouched down so we were facing eye-to-eye, and I resisted the urge to pull him down onto the bed.

"You say it like it's a bad thing."

He smiled. "Isn't it? I've been down this road before. It didn't end well for me. Or her."

Pain slashed across his face. I reached out and touched his cheek, and he leaned into my touch. "I'm not human."

"You're close enough," he retorted. "In *their* eyes, at least."

"Castiel," I whispered, and his eyes focused back in on me. "I want..."

"Tell me," he said. "I need you to tell me."

I told him. Not in so many words, but I told him. Pulling him to me, I pressed my lips against his. Careful at first, unsure. Then he breathed me in, capturing my lips with a hunger I had never experienced before. He crawled on top of me, his hands caressing my neck, my jaw. Opening my lips for him, I finally got to taste him. I wrapped my arms around his neck, pulling him closer still. He was heavy on top of me, in the most delicious way, and I needed more. I needed *him*.

Castiel pulled back, but before I could protest, his lips were on my jaw, then he nipped and sucked at the sensitive skin on my neck. I gasped as pleasure rolled through me, and a low moan escaped him at my reaction. I wrapped my legs around his body, and Castiel pressed down, making sure I could feel just how much he needed me, too.

"Do you have any idea what you do to me?" he

asked between kisses. "What you do to my mind? My body?"

"I'm starting to think I do," I teased, smiling as he pressed a sweet kiss to my lips again. Castiel groaned as I arched up against him, and his fingers made their way to the edge of my shirt. He touched the soft skin on my stomach, bunched the fabric in his hands as he pulled the shirt higher.

"I need to see you," he breathed out.

I helped him get my shirt over my head, and the way he gazed down at me was enough to make me blush again. Castiel ran one thumb over my bra, feeling the hardened nub underneath the fabric.

"So beautiful," he said, his voice coarse and rough. "Do you know how beautiful you are, Danika?"

I didn't answer that. There was no need. "Kiss me again."

He did. Oh, how he kissed me again. Castiel threaded his fingers in with mine, lifting my arms up and pinning them over my head. I squirmed underneath him as he kissed his way down my body.

"As soon as we're alone," he said, breathless. "Then I will show you just how much I want you."

A tinge of disappointment settled in my stomach. I wanted him to show me right then and there. But at the same time, Micah's mother's guest room was probably not the place for things to go any further.

"Then we better find a place to be alone," I said. Castiel raised his head and smirked at me.

"Yeah? Tell me, what do you want me to do to you? Once we're alone."

I bit my bottom lip. "I just want you."

His amused expression softened into something else. He raised himself up over me and looked down at my face. There was such affection there that I almost forgot how to breathe.

"I want you, too," he whispered. "I probably shouldn't, but I do."

He leaned back down and pressed a kiss to my lips. He then settled next to me on the bed, holding me close. "Will you stay with me tonight?" I asked.

"If you want me to."

"Do *you* want to?"

Castiel smiled. "What do you think?"

I smiled back, then rested my head on his chest. He held me in his arms, and I listened to the steady beating of his heart. I liked this. I wanted more of this. Somewhere quiet, where we didn't have to look over our shoulders every second of the day. Just me and him.

Perhaps a place in the city so I could stay close to my sisters. I swallowed down the lump in my throat. I knew that wasn't going to happen. Castiel was going to be an angel soon enough, and we were still hiding out. I couldn't see a happy ending for us.

I shoved the thought aside. Might as well enjoy the time we *did* have together. However brief it may be.

Somewhere downstairs, I heard Micah's voice. He sounded stressed, and I looked at Castiel. "Do you hear that?" I asked. He nodded.

"Something's wrong."

My stomach dropped.

Suddenly, I heard his footsteps running up the stairs. I got up and had just gotten my shirt back in place when the door swung open.

"You two better come," Micah said, his eyes wide open. "They're outside."

CHAPTER 16

Running downstairs, we found Vera standing in front of a window, looking outside. I did the same, seeing a handful of angels through the window, circling the area in the sky. Despite everything, I felt a small sense of relief. I had expected to find them barging through the door.

"I don't think they know we're here," I said.

"Maybe not," Castiel replied. "But they're far too close for my liking."

I looked up at him. "Maybe we should leave. I don't want to risk them coming in."

"Nonsense," Vera told us. "The house is hidden from them; they cannot find it. Stay until they move on."

"She's right," Castiel said. "This is the safest place right now."

"Just keep an eye on them," Micah chimed in, giving his mother a worried look. "If the protection spell fails—"

"Why would it fail?" Vera asked. "It has held strong for years and years. They might not even be here on your behalf; angels are everywhere these days."

Well, she was right about that. I didn't recognize the ones outside, but they weren't close enough to get a proper look. Castiel took my hand, his warm skin calming my racing heart. There was nothing for us to do but wait them out.

"Danika and I can keep watch," Castiel said after Vera yawned three times within five minutes. "We'll come get you if something happens."

"Thank you, dear," Vera said and patted him on the arm. "I really don't think there's anything to worry about."

Micah looked less certain. "Are you sure? I can stay up with you guys."

"No need," Castiel told him. "Get some rest."

Micah nodded and gave me one last look. I nodded also, hoping he would leave us alone. His nervous energy only made me more skittish.

Once we were alone, Castiel turned to me.

"Can you go upstairs and get our things? Just in case we have to leave."

I nodded and hurried up the stairs. I quickly gathered my things, and then I moved on to Castiel's room. There were some clothes that had fallen out of his bag. He must've been rummaging through it earlier. I stuffed them back in and felt something hard.

The metal box.

I looked over my shoulder, but there was no one close to me. I knew I shouldn't, knew he wanted it to stay private for a reason. But I needed to know what was so important.

I opened it.

At first, it seemed insignificant. A simple necklace with a thin gold chain. The front of the charm that hung from the chain had been engraved with Sydney's name. I smiled. Probably a gift from Castiel. It was most likely the only thing he had left of her. I fumbled a little as I tried to close the box, and the charm flipped over. I reached to turn it right when I saw that it had been engraved on the back as well. I frowned at the words.

Sydney,
You have my heart.
Gabriel.

Gabriel? I didn't understand. Did Gabriel give her this necklace? It didn't make any sense. My head was spinning. What was Castiel not telling me? I slammed the box shut and hurried back downstairs. Castiel stood right where I had left him, looking out the window. He looked over his shoulder when he heard me come back downstairs, and when he saw the anger on my face, he turned to me fully.

"What's wrong?"

"You tell me!" I practically yelled and shoved the box into his hands. The color drained from his face when he realized what he was holding.

"You opened it?"

"Don't give me any shit over that!" I snapped. "Yes, I opened it. What does it mean? Why does it say that it's from Gabriel to Sydney? I don't understand."

Castiel dragged a hand over his face, a sigh escaping him. "I couldn't let him have it," he said. "When I saw the box in his hand that day, I just..."

"You just what?" I asked. "Please, tell me what this means."

At first, I didn't think he was going to tell me. But then he nodded and opened his mouth to speak. "He loved her first." It looked like it pained him to say it, but Castiel didn't stop talking. "And she loved him. Gabriel can be very charming, and he loves fiercely. But he is also cruel and jealous. I caught him with her one night and saw the way he treated her. I threatened to report him—they'd have his wings if they found out. So, he threatened to kill her if I did. I couldn't let that happen. I took her away. Hid her. And I fell in love."

I was stunned. It felt like someone had struck me with a metal rod across the head. "And she fell for you, too."

"Yes. Gabriel found us eventually, of course.

Reported me and got her killed. If he couldn't have her, no one could."

"Didn't you say that he had been with her, too?" I asked. "Why does he still have his wings?"

Castiel huffed out a humorless laugh. "As if anyone would believe me. Gabriel is an archangel. And besides, I had just been reported by him. No one would believe a word coming out of my mouth if I so much as hinted at him having done the same thing."

I guessed that made sense. "Why didn't you tell me?"

Castiel shook his head. "At first, because I didn't know if I could trust you. And now..." He cupped my cheek. "I got scared. I didn't want you to think any less of me."

"Why would I think any less of you? Castiel, you did the right thing. Taking her out of that situation. It's not your fault that the laws are so messed up. I only wished you hadn't lied to me."

He leaned down and pressed a light kiss to my lips. "I'm sorry. This is... difficult. I feel like I'm betraying her for wanting you."

"You're not," I assured him. "It's been eight years. Wouldn't she want you to find someone again?"

"Yes," he said. "I suppose she would."

"If she was as kind as you'd said, then I'm sure she would."

"And it doesn't bother you?" he asked. "She will always be a part of me."

"I understand that. But that doesn't mean you can't

care for me, too. I'm a different person. It won't be the same kind of..." I almost said love. "The same kind of affection."

I couldn't read the expression on Castiel's face. But I thought it was happiness I saw there, behind the hurt and worry.

"You're pretty amazing, you know that?"

I smiled. "Oh, I'm the best."

He kissed me again, knocking the wind out of me, and I held onto his arms. As we broke apart, his nose bumped against mine.

"We should probably keep an eye on what's going on outside," he said.

The angels were still circling the same spot. I frowned. It sort of looked like they were giant birds circling in on their prey.

"Do you think they're here for someone else?" I asked. "A Nephila or something."

"Maybe," Castiel said. He also seemed to think their behavior was strange.

Soon, the angels dove straight for the ground. I flinched, hoping my theory was incorrect. But I was almost certain that an innocent Nephila had been their target. I knew I couldn't do anything to help; I was too far away. But knowing that someone was dying—right there out in the open—sickened me.

"I think we should get out," Castiel said. "They're distracted. We might not get another chance."

"Take the heli."

We whirled around, just in time for Micah to toss Castiel the key to the aircraft.

"Are you sure?" I asked. Micah nodded.

"Of course. Castiel's right. You should get out now when their focus is elsewhere."

We grabbed our bags, and I stopped in front of Micah. "Thank you," I said and kissed him on the cheek. "You're a real friend."

He sighed, a teasing grin on his lips. "Ah, always the bridesmaid, never the bride." He turned to Castiel. "You keep her safe, okay?"

"Always."

Castiel shook his hand, and then Very stepped out into the living room. "What's this I hear about leaving?"

"It might be our only shot for a while," Castiel explained. "But thank you for letting us stay. And don't worry." A look passed between them that I suspected had something to do with their conversation from before. Vera nodded.

"I won't. Thank you for speaking with me last night. You've put my mind at rest."

We both gave Vera a quick hug before we ran outside. Hand-in-hand, we hurried toward the aircraft that was parked just a few streets away, and within minutes, we were in the air.

"Do you know where we should go?" I asked. Castiel nodded.

"I know a place that's secluded. We'll go there."

He turned the vehicle around so we were heading

in the opposite direction from where the angels were. I strapped myself in, and I kept looking behind us, half-expecting to see a whole swarm appear. But we managed to get out of the city unscathed.

When I could no longer see the city lights, I slumped back, able to relax a little. It was a silent journey, and my head was spinning with everything that had happened over the past few days. I hoped Micah would stay with his mother, at least for a while. Even if I could understand his unwillingness to let me help him, I also wished he would've let me take his powers. It would mean that he'd be safe. Saf*er*, at least.

I glanced at Castiel, who drove the heli in silent concentration. Perhaps it worked differently than the one he used to have; he didn't seem quite as comfortable behind the steering levers. But I was grateful that I didn't have to drive. I couldn't concentrate enough for that.

A small thrill went through me at the thought of him earlier. Lying on top of me, marking me with his kisses. His strong hands exploring my body, his soft skin and strong arms holding me. I bit my lip, trying to hide my smile. It wasn't the time to think about things like that. We were running away, for crying out loud! But even still, his words echoed in my mind.

As soon as we're alone, then I will show you just how much I want you.

I really hoped he would get a chance to show me just that.

CHAPTER 17

After a while, I thought I could recognize the landscape outside the heli. In the distance, I noticed a familiar sight. The silhouette of my home in the early morning light. My city. I turned to him.

"Are you sure we should be here?"

Castiel nodded. "We won't go into the actual city just yet. I don't think Gabriel and his people expect us so close to home. We should be safe here for a little while if we're careful enough."

It was a smart strategy. The angels were probably

still looking for us closer to where we shook them off last time. Castiel slowly made the aircraft descend, and we touched the ground right behind an old, abandoned ruin of some kind. I had never seen it before, but it seemed familiar to Castiel.

"What is this place?"

"It used to be a church," he explained. "It must've been built hundreds of years ago. Not much left of it now."

"We can sleep in the heli," I said. "This church is big enough to hide it, I think." At least, what was left of the church. I remembered my grandfather telling me about such places. About the high ceilings and stone floors. The music and art that could be experienced inside. I wondered what it looked like once upon a time.

"Can we explore it?" I asked, and Castiel nodded.

"I don't see why not."

It wasn't very big. There was something that looked like an altar of some sort at one end of the structure, but most of it had been torn down. Stone steps that led to nowhere. Two of the walls were still standing, and remnants of colored glass were still on the high windows. Everything else was gone.

"I've never been in a church before," I told him.

"Not many of them left." He looked up at the altar. "They used to be quite beautiful, though."

"I bet."

His hand took hold of mine, and he brought it to his lips. "We should probably check out the area. Do you think you can set up some sort of barrier around here? Just something to ward the goons off if they should come?"

"Of course," I said with a nod. We went back outside, and while Castiel looked around the area, I got to work with a shielding spell. Nothing as powerful as the one that had protected Vera's house, but it was better than nothing.

"It looks like we're alone out here," he said when he finally came back. "I think we should try and get some food. I think I saw some sort of animal not too far from here."

I laughed. "Maybe I should go hunting then if we're to get any food before sundown."

"If that's a jab at the time I tried to catch a fish, then—"

"Oh, it's definitely a jab at that." I patted his arm. "Get a fire started, and I'll see what I can find."

He smiled and shook his head at me. "The only reason you even caught that fish was because of your magic."

"Yeah, yeah," I said and waved him off. "More fire, less talking. Be right back."

I could see a cluster of trees and bushes a bit further ahead, and I figured that would be my best chance at finding something for us to eat. The sun didn't reach through the thick bushel of leaves above, so it almost felt like it was going from day to night within a matter of seconds.

My eyes soon got used to the dim light, and I

stopped for a minute, trying to see if there were any animals around. At first, I didn't see anything, although I could hear birds chirping. There had to be at least a rabbit or squirrel around here somewhere!

Then I heard a sound that I didn't recognize. A chuckling noise coming from the serene place under the trees.

There it was again! I pulled my blade out, looking around. Then I saw the strangest bird, right there on the path in front of me. The movements were jerky and erratic, and it moved its head this way and that. The feathers were a mix of green and blue, dark in its tone. It wasn't very beautiful, but it looked fat and plump.

Before it could run away, I tethered it to the ground with my magic. It didn't take much to keep such a small creature in place—it barely reached my mid-calf when I walked up to it. To my surprise, it didn't make its strange chuckling sound when I came near it. It just looked at me with its black, beady eyes. I took a deep breath. For some reason, this wasn't as easy as spearing the fish. Still, it had to be done. We needed to eat.

"Sorry about this, little friend," I said quietly, and then I reached out for it.

It only took one swift swipe of my blade to kill it, and I swallowed down the bile that rose in my throat. I *definitely* didn't have what it took to live like this. What I wouldn't give for a nicely stocked grocery store.

The bird was heavy in my hand when I carried it back to Castiel, who had gotten a fire started. It probably wasn't smart to have a fire going in case the smoke gave us away, but we very well couldn't eat the bird raw. We'd just have to make quick work of it, then put the fire out as soon as we finished eating.

"Look at this!" I called out and raised the bird up in the air. "Aren't you impressed?"

Castiel chuckled. "Very. You're a regular cavewoman."

I handed him the bird, and he got to work cleaning it. There were green and blue feathers everywhere, carried away by the wind. Castiel had prepared some kindle to use when cooking the bird, and soon, we had the juicy, white meat ready. It didn't taste like much without any spices, but I was so hungry that I didn't care.

We sat right next to each other, picking at the meat, a companionable silence stretching between us. I wondered if he was thinking about his wings. His powers. I thought this place might be good for doing the spell. I wanted to help him, but I also would miss this version of Castiel. The human one.

Well, he could never be fully human, I suppose. There was something about him that made him so much more. It wasn't just the fact that he was really an angel. It was something else, something that skirted the edge of darkness underneath the surface. Perhaps it was there because of everything he'd lived through. Losing his wings. Losing Sydney. But there was light, too. Light and a sense of safety that I hadn't experienced with anyone else. He noticed me watching him and smiled.

"What?"

I shook my head. "Nothing. I was just thinking."

He wiped his hands on the grass beneath us, then wrapped an arm around my waist. "Tell me what's on your mind."

I smiled, then leaned my head on his shoulder. "It's nothing important."

"Okay," he said. "You can still tell me if you want."

"No, I don't want to talk about it."

Castiel put a finger under my chin, tilting my head up so I was looking at him. "What do you want to do then?"

Amusement danced in his eyes. I tilted my head further, my face just inches from him. I didn't need to say it. He knew what I wanted. Closeness. Warmth. His lips on mine.

The kiss was soft. Feathery light and slow. When we finally broke apart, he leaned his forehead against mine.

"We should put the fire out," he said quietly.

I nodded. I knew he was right. But in that moment, all I wanted to do was stop time. To just have one minute like this. With him. No outside world. No angels. No threat. Just him and me.

But that wasn't reality.

I put the fire out with my magic, suffocating the flames. When that was done, we got back into the heli. It had started to rain, and the droplets splattered against the vehicle's windows. It was actually kind of cozy. We made room in the back of the aircraft, spreading out a blanket that Castiel had found in the storage compartment.

We then lied down, looking up at the sky through the top window. My hand searched for his, and he took it, bringing it to his chest. I could feel the beating of his heart, even through his shirt. I glanced over at him, smiling.

"Are you nervous?" I asked.

Castiel shook his head. "No. Why do you ask?"

"Your heart. It's beating really fast."

He turned on his side to face me. "It is. But that's because you're here."

"I don't make you nervous?" I asked, turning to face him. Castiel shook his head.

"No. Not nervous."

"Then what?"

He pulled a strand of hair out of my face. "You drive me fucking wild."

And then he kissed me.

CHAPTER 18

I dragged him on top of me, never breaking our kiss. He was eager to comply, and soon, I had his delicious weight between my legs again. I couldn't get close enough, needed to feel *all* of him. I tugged at Castiel's shirt, and he lifted himself up so that I could pull it over his head.

I swore under my breath at the sight of his bare chest, and he chuckled lightly at my reaction to him. His laughter died in his throat when I caught his lips again, swiping at his bottom lip with my tongue until he let me in. The kiss deepened, and his hands softly explored my body. Caressed my arms, then down to my hips. He grabbed hold of my shirt, and I could feel his skin against my own when he flung it to the side. I reached between us, finding the button of his pants.

"I want you out of these," I whispered, lips still pressed to his. "Now."

I felt him smile, and then he sat up on his knees, his eyes firmly on me. Slowly, he unbuttoned his pants, never breaking eye contact. He unzipped his fly, and I swallowed at the sight of the bulge that strained against the fabric.

Castiel got onto his feet, although he had to stay crouched down in the cramped space. He kicked his shoes off and then the pants. He hooked his thumbs in the waistband of his boxer briefs, and they soon joined the rest of his clothes. Castiel sat back down in front of me, completely naked. I felt my cheeks heat at the sight of him. Especially at the sight of the hard length that I longed to touch.

"Your turn," he growled before getting me just as naked.

Leaning down over my bare body, he kissed every inch of exposed skin. Taking one breast into his mouth, his tongue swirling around the hard nipple, one of his hands caressing the other breast. I arched against his touch, moaning as he bit down gently over the sensitive nipple. Castiel's smile when he let go was wicked, like he had only just begun making me writhe beneath him.

"Castiel," I panted. "I need you."

"Patience," he teased, looking far too pleased with

torturing me. I glare at him, which only made him laugh. "Don't worry," he said, kissing his way down my stomach. "I'm far too greedy to not touch you."

Before I could say another word, he started to kiss my inner thighs. He touched my hot core next, making me cry out as he reached my most sensitive part. I felt one of his fingers enter me, and then he put his mouth on me, and I almost came. I held him steady with my hands in his hair, needing him *right there.*

"Just like that," I whispered, breathless as his tongue swiped over me. I could feel him tense his hips as he worked me over, and I couldn't wait to have him back between my thighs, filling me completely.

"Fuck, you taste good," he muttered, working his finger inside of me. "I want to see you come, Danika."

"I'm close," I panted, and when he put his mouth back on me, I felt the sensation build inside of me. I felt it spread through my entire body until I finally fell over the edge. I cried out as my orgasm shook me, and Castiel watched me with reverence in his eyes as I slowly fell down from my high.

"So beautiful."

I propped myself up onto my elbows, feeling utterly boneless. "Come here," I said, not done with him just yet.

Castiel crawled back up over me, settling between my legs. I spread them wide, wrapping my legs around his body. I could feel his hardness as he rolled his hips against me, so close to where I really wanted him. He kissed me hard and fierce, none of the gentleness and restraint from before there anymore.

"I need you inside me," I whispered against his lips.

Castiel groaned and kissed my neck, bit down on the skin there as he aligned himself against my opening. I gasped as he pushed in, and for a moment, neither of us moved.

The delicious burn soon turned into a sensitive pleasure, and I started moving my hips to let him know I was ready. Castiel moved slowly at first, dragging himself in and out while kissing me. But soon, it was like he couldn't hold back anymore. His movements became more erratic, more desperate, and within a few minutes, I was holding onto him as he thrust into me. Hard and fast and so *good*.

"Fuck," he growled. "You're incredible. You feel so amazing, Danika. I'm close. So fucking close."

He reached between us, finding just the right spot, and with just a few swipes of his finger in tandem with his thrusts, I came again. Clamping around him, holding on for dear life, I let the orgasm roll through me. Castiel followed soon after. His entire body stiffened, and his cry was muffled when he buried his face into my neck.

We rested there for several minutes, just catching our breath. I couldn't stop smiling. Couldn't stop touching his strong arms and back. Then he finally rolled off of me, kissing me deeply. Castiel smiled, his eyes sparkling when he pulled me close.

"How are you feeling?" he asked and kissed my temple. I smiled and looked up at him.

"Wonderful. I feel wonderful. How about you?"

He didn't answer right away. Just watched me, and I could practically hear the wheels turning in his head. "Conflicted."

"Why?"

"I suppose I'm torn between wanting two things." He stroked my arm absently with his fingers. "Becoming who I used to be, and remaining who I am right now. With you."

I felt a lump form in my throat. "Does it have to be two sides of you? Do you have to choose?"

Castiel nodded. "I can't risk hurting you, Danika. I've—"

"You've been down this road before, I know." I got up in a half-sitting position and looked down at him. I stroked the deep lines on his forehead until he relaxed. "But this situation is different. The angels already want me dead. With or without you, I'm in danger."

He nodded. "Yes, I suppose you are."

"And it's like you said when we first met," I continued. "Isn't it better that I have an angel on my side? Do you remember?"

"I remember. But it won't be an easy life."

"I know. But I'd rather have a hard life with you than an easy life on my own."

"You won't be able to go back to your coven."

Something stabbed at my heart when I heard the words spoken out loud. I had come to that conclusion myself already, however, and it wasn't enough to deter me. "No, I won't."

"And that's alright with you?" he asked. "You love your sisters."

"I do." *So* much. But maybe I wouldn't have been able to go back regardless of whether I was with Castiel or not. The angels already attacked them once. If I returned... it could be bad.

"As long as you're sure," Castiel said and pulled me down for a kiss. "I couldn't live with myself if I knew I was the reason for your unhappiness."

"You could never be that. Despite everything, you only bring me happiness," I replied, cupping his face. I loved the way his stubble under my thumb felt as I stroked his jaw.

"Good," he whispered with a soft smile. "Because I'm starting to believe that you are the key to my happiness, too."

We lied there, just talking for hours. For a moment, I wished we didn't have to move, didn't have to return to reality. But of course, we did. After getting dressed, we decided to head outside.

"So, you're sure you still want to help me?" Castiel asked. I nodded.

"Of course. If this is what you want, then I will try to help you."

He took my face gently between his hands and kissed me. "Thank you, Danika. You don't know what this means to me."

"Should we do it now?" I asked. "We're alone in a secluded spot. Seems ideal to me."

He took one shuddering breath before he nodded. "Okay. Let's do it."

My pulse was rushing through my body as I placed myself in front of him. I still wasn't sure I could do it, but I was at least going to try. "It might be uncomfortable," I said. "It might even hurt."

"I can handle it," Castiel muttered, jaw squared and eyes hard. "Don't hold back."

I took a deep breath, then took his hand and placed it over his heart. I had my hand over his, and I held onto his arm with my other one, needing to feel him there. Strong and steady.

I closed my eyes and called on my magic. I hoped this would work. I figured that it should work in a similar way as when I helped the Nephilim. Only the other way around. I really didn't have a blueprint to follow, so I could only hope that I was on the right track. I spoke the ancient words and reached inside.

Somewhere deep within Castiel, I found a darkness. I quickly realized that it was his angelic soul. It was still there but blackened. Transformed. I frowned. He was a good man. Sure, there was something in his eyes when he fought; I had seen it when he killed those angels. Something feral and dark. But *this*? It was just... wrong.

I lured it out from the shadows, and Castiel gasped. My grip on him tightened, keeping him steady. I pulled on the power within him, lying dormant in there.

Together with his angelic power, I started to transform the blackness of his soul. Little by little, slowly but surely.

I felt tremors go through his body, but I didn't open my eyes. He said he could handle the pain, the discomfort, and I believed him. So, I kept pushing.

It was a little different from taking the powers from the Nephilim. Instead of severing the ties, I mended them. I just hoped I put them together the right way. Castiel grunted in pain, but he stayed put.

"It's working," he managed to get out. "I can feel it working."

I wasn't sure how he could know that, but his words of encouragement were enough to keep me going. I felt sweat running down my back from the effort, but I ignored it. It wouldn't be much longer— only a few more loose ends to put together.

"Danika, stop!"

The fear in Castiel's voice was just a product of what was happening, I told myself. Having his whole being altered was no easy thing. I kept going. He grunted, and then he jerked back. I opened my eyes, confusion clouding my mind for a second. Then I felt strange hands grabbing my arms, and I was jerked back, too. Castiel was being held down by three angels, and a chill ran through me when a familiar voice spoke into my ear.

"Interfering with heavenly business, are we? You never did know when to stop, witch."

Gabriel.

CHAPTER 19

"Castiel!" I cried out. I could barely see him; the others were dragging him away.

He must be weaker from the spell. Otherwise, he would fight back. Our eyes met for a second, and I saw a glazed-over look. He was about to pass out. Gabriel turned me around so that I faced him.

"Your precious Castiel will never be the angel he once was," he growled, his voice far too calm and soft for what he was saying. "I hope you realize that."

I spat him right in the face. "Let me go."

Gabriel wiped his cheek with one hand, the other

firmly placed around my upper arm. I needed to act. Needed to get away. But my powers were depleted, run into the ground after I attempted to mend Castiel's angelic form. I felt like I could barely stand.

"Now, what am I to do with you?" he mused as if I were some disobedient child he had caught with her hand in the cookie jar. "Time after time again, you go against Heaven's rules. You help the tainted children. And now, you've attempted to restore an angel that had already fallen." He tutted and shook his head. "Quite the rulebreaker, aren't you? More trouble than you're worth, to be completely honest."

"I know what you did," I said, my voice breaking on the words. "I know what you did to Sydney. You killed her!"

"Of course, I did," he said dryly. "She had mingled with an angel, tainted our bloodline."

I frowned. "Your bloodline?"

"Oh, he didn't tell you?" Gabriel smirked. " Sydney was pregnant when I put her out of her misery."

That evil, miserable bastard. "Did he know?"

Gabriel shrugged. "Maybe he didn't, come to think of it. It doesn't matter. She's dead, and soon, you will be, too. Castiel really has some bad luck with those he chooses to love."

"What will happen to him?"

"Well, he obviously can't be trusted to live out his life down here. He'll be locked up; it's for the best."

So, Gabriel *wasn't* going to kill him. Interesting.

"You sure do talk a lot," I said. "If you're going to kill me, just do it."

Amusement flashed across Gabriel's face. "Are we so eager to die? I'm afraid I can't oblige. Not yet."

"I don't understand."

"Of course, you don't," he tutted again. "You are to be brought to Heaven, where they will decide how you shall die. You have done far too much to our kind for me to just kill you where you stand."

He wrapped an arm around my waist, and try as I might, I couldn't free myself. He couldn't be serious, right? He wasn't actually going to take me to Heaven.

Further ahead, I saw the other angels take off with Castiel. And not two seconds later, Gabriel spread his massive wings and took off toward the sky. The wind tore at my skin, my eyes watering from the speed.

I couldn't scream. Couldn't do anything. Was I going into shock? Nothing seemed to work, no matter how hard I tried to access my magic. This wasn't just burnout; this was something else.

Gabriel ascended quickly, and after a while, we broke through some sort of barrier. I gasped for air, trying to remain calm as he landed. Looking around, there wasn't another soul in sight. Was this really Heaven? It looked like a city, maybe a bit cleaner.

The closer I looked, I saw that the buildings seemed to be made out of glass. Gabriel grabbed my arm and started walking, leaving me no choice but to follow. More angels were milling around the further we went into the city. He had his eyes set on an impressive building straight ahead. It seemed endlessly big, reaching high up in the sky.

Inside was a flurry of activities, with angels all around. I even saw female angels, something I had never seen back home. I wasn't even aware they existed. Strange. I couldn't gawk at them for long because Gabriel dragged me behind him to a massive set of doors. He pushed them open, moving like he owned the place. At the end of the room was a table, angels filling every chair around it.

"Here she is now," Gabriel said and threw me in front of the others. I stumbled but found my footing soon after. They all looked at me like I was something unpleasant that had gotten stuck to the underside of their shoe.

"Are you the witch, Danika Ryker?" the man at the far end of the table asked.

"Who's asking?" I snapped, and his eyes turned dark.

"Michael, archangel of Heaven. Now, answer my question."

Michael? I had heard of him but never met him myself. He looked slightly older than Gabriel, his dark hair speckled with gray at the temples. There was a severeness about his mouth that made him look like he was constantly smelling something unpleasant. Something told me this man was not used to being opposed.

I straightened. "Yeah, I'm her."

"And you are aware that you have broken many of our laws?"

"Your laws are not mine."

He leaned forward in his seat. "*Answer me.*"

"Yes," I said and rolled my eyes. "I am aware."

"Very well," he replied and looked at Gabriel. "Put her away until we decide what to do with her."

"What's there to decide?" Gabriel asked. "Kill her, brother."

"I will not ask you again," Michael huffed, a warning to his voice. "Take her away."

I wondered if they had some sort of prison somewhere. For some reason, that struck me as ridiculous. A heavenly prison just didn't sound right. But I suspected that was exactly where I was being taken.

Gabriel gave his brother a death glare, but then took my arm in his firm grip again and dragged me out of the room. We walked down some stairs, then went through seemingly endless corridors until we reached a row of cells. They seemed empty, but the place was dark, so I couldn't really see all that well.

He dragged me over to the one on the far end of the room, and after telling the guard on post to leave, he threw me into the cell. I stumbled, just barely able to stay on my feet. Before I could even think about running toward the open cell door, he slammed it shut and made a big show of locking it.

"How long am I supposed to sit down here?" I called out to him as he started to leave. Gabriel turned and looked at me with his cold, blue eyes.

"As long as we see fit," he taunted, even though I could see on his face that he was annoyed with his brother's decision to put me in a cell. If it was just Gabriel, I would've been dead already.

"And Castiel?" I asked, clutching the bars of my cell. "What happened to him?"

Gabriel stood in front of me, a look of pure disgust on his face. "I don't understand him," he huffed, ignoring my question. "Why stoop so low and be with a human?"

"I'm not human," I pointed out. "And besides, you did it, too."

Gabriel's eyes narrowed. "Do not speak of things you don't understand, witch."

"What is there to understand? You loved her."

"I did *not*."

I scoffed at him. What a sad creature he was. As much a prisoner of his own laws as the rest of them. He couldn't even acknowledge his love for Sydney to me without any other angel listening.

"Then why did you give her that necklace?" I asked, tilting my head to the side. Gabriel looked just about ready to strangle me through the bars.

"Careful, witch. You're way in over your head."

"*Sydney*," I quoted. "*You have my heart. Gabriel.*"

"One more word..."

"Wasn't that what it said?" I asked, ignoring the fury in his eyes. "I believe it was."

He slammed his fist against one of the cell bars, making the entire front rattle. I couldn't help but flinch at the sudden movement. Gabriel pointed a finger right at my face. "I shall kill you myself, make no mistake. I shall enjoy watching the life leave your eyes. And I shall make *him* watch."

Him? So, Castiel was here somewhere, too. A strange sense of relief came over me. At least he wasn't dead. Yet.

"Did you enjoy killing her, too?" I asked. He was already royally pissed off. I might as well keep fanning that fire. Inflict pain where I could.

"I did," he growled, a wicked grin on his face. "She betrayed me when she opened her legs for that sorry excuse of an angel. Yes, I enjoyed killing her immensely."

Sick bastard.

He gave me one final look, then turned on his heel and walked away. His steps echoed on the marble floor, and I sank down onto my knees. My legs just didn't carry me any longer. I took a deep breath, trying to ward off the panic. I was in Heaven. I was locked up, awaiting my sentence.

And I had no idea where Castiel was. That was what got to me the most. If I could just see him, then I wouldn't imagine the worst. But it was strange that he wasn't in one of these cells also. They were just empty. I couldn't imagine there being *more* cells somewhere. How many prisoners did Heaven really take?

Where was he?

CHAPTER 20

I didn't know how long I'd sat there on the hard floor of the cell. Time seemed to have lost its meaning. So, when I finally heard footsteps, I quickly got on my feet. Was this going to be it? Would they kill me without letting me see Castiel first? Never in my life had I missed having my magic as I did in that moment. Not being able to defend myself was a horrible feeling.

I expected to see some guards come for me, or even Gabriel. But when Michael walked down the stairs to the cells, I have to admit that I was a bit surprised. I'd think he was too high and mighty to come visit Heaven's prisoners.

"Danika Ryker," he said in greeting. When I didn't answer, he continued. "You are to be brought before my council, but I wanted to have a word with you first."

"I have nothing to say to you," I hissed, backing away a few steps from the bars. Michael's mouth showed that severe look again. *Definitely* not used to being opposed.

"But I have some things to say to you first. I suggest you listen." There was no room for argument in his tone. Michael raised his chin and watched me with those hooded eyes of his. He clasped his hands together in front of his body. "How many of the Nephilim have you helped escape?"

I frowned. He really wanted to talk about the Nephilim? "I don't know."

"Give me an estimate."

I shrugged. "I really don't know. I help as many as I can. Less than I would've liked, though."

"Why help them?" Michael asked. "I don't know a single witch who would do such a thing."

I couldn't hold back a laugh. "Of course not. There's a lot of bad blood between the angels and the witches. Not to mention the fact that they would get on your bad side if they helped the Nephilim."

"And that was never a concern for you?"

I shook my head. "No, it wasn't. What you do to the Nephilim is sick. They never asked to be born. It's the least I can do if my magic can give them a normal life."

"But they are not normal," Michael told me. "And it's not up to you to interfere with Heaven's business. My brother, Gabriel, tells me you have a tendency to do just that."

I straightened. "As often as I can."

Michael hummed in displeasure. "I see. And then there's the matter of the fallen. Castiel."

I felt my body stiffen at the mention of his name. "Where is he?"

Michael pursed his lips. "Around. You'll see him soon enough. There are some... interesting developments regarding him."

Interesting developments. What the *fuck* did that even mean? "I don't understand."

"My brothers tell me that you were performing a spell on him when they found you," Michael said. "As I understand it, you were attempting to restore his wings as well as his former powers."

I didn't answer that. I didn't need to. Michael saw the answer written all over my face. He nodded slowly, then turned his gaze to the staircase. He called out a name, and one of the guards came running in.

"Take her to the council room," Michael ordered. "We'll be waiting for her."

The guard nodded, and Michael disappeared up the stairs. I shrank back when the guard opened the cell door, a pair of shackles in his hands. They were really going to be using those on me? I got my answer soon enough when he slapped them around my wrists and tugged me along after him.

The eyes of every angel we passed were fixed on me. The guard walked briskly, and I had to do a sort of half jog just to keep up. When he finally stopped in front of a massive pair of doors, I was completely out of breath. He knocked once, then opened them.

Inside were the same people I had seen before, where I had first seen Michael. Gabriel was seated next to him, and if looks could kill, I'd be a puddle on the floor right then.

"There she is," Michael said as if we hadn't just spoken moments ago. "Bring her to the stand, please."

The guard dragged me to a small, raised part of the floor in front of them all. Like a miniature stage where they could get a good look at me.

"Bring out the other prisoner," Michael commanded.

I looked around, frantically trying to see what was happening. The other prisoner. Did that mean Castiel? Would we be put in front of the council together? Maybe it would be as Gabriel said. That they were going to make Castiel watch as they killed me. I hoped at least some of my spell had worked. That he would have at least a semblance of his powers again. Maybe we could get out.

When the doors flung open, my heart was beating so fast in my chest that I thought it might just fall out. First, I only saw the guard.

Then I saw Castiel.

I gasped. He was bloodied and beaten, his wrists bound together with the same shackles mine were in. But it wasn't the blood that had me the most shocked. It was his eyes. They were black as night. Not just the iris, but they were *completely* black. What had they done to him? A thought hit me. Or was this because of me? Because I hadn't finished the spell!

"Castiel!" I shouted, and his head snapped up.

Those black eyes seemed to see right into the deepest parts of my soul. He didn't say anything as the guard positioned him on a similar raised part of the floor as the one I stood on. Just hung his head, eyes staring straight ahead.

"Now that you're both here, we can begin."

I heard Michael's voice from the head of the table, but I didn't see him. I couldn't look away from Castiel.

"After some careful deliberation," Michael continued, "the council has decided that you both shall die for your crimes. You will be brought to a cell while everything is being prepared. Are there any last words you would like to say?"

Castiel said nothing. I tore my eyes from him and looked at the archangel. "What's with all this? The formality. You all knew we were going to die before we even got to Heaven. Why drag it out?"

"It is how things are done," Michael simply stated, his tone clipped. "If there's nothing else..."

He waved his hand at the guards, and we were both taken away. They seemed to be taking us to the same place this time, for which I was strangely grateful.

They threw us into neighboring cells, and while I couldn't see him, at least I knew he was there.

"Castiel!" I called out. "Please, talk to me. What did they do to you?"

No answer.

A terrible thought hit me. What if he didn't understand me? What if he had been so altered that he had become something else altogether? A monster, devoid of thoughts and feelings?

I clutched at the bars, pressing my face against them in hopes of getting a glimpse of him. I could barely see his hands wrapped around the bars of his cell, his knuckles white as snow.

"Castiel?" I tried to get a better look, but I couldn't. "What happened to you?"

No answer.

"Do you understand me?" I asked, fighting back the tears that threatened to well over.

"Yes."

About time. "Are you alright?"

"Something's wrong." He didn't say anything else, and I felt panic rise within me.

"Because of what we tried to do?" I asked. "Tell me what's happening."

"I can feel... *something*. It's moving around inside of me."

Oh, no. I knew I should've never attempted to change him back. The blackened part of his soul was still in there. I didn't cleanse it entirely before the angels came. Was that what was moving around in there? A creature in its own right?

"I can't do anything!" I cried, my voice shaking. "I can't access my magic here."

"No," he said. "Your magic is no good here."

"Castiel, I'm sorry. I'm so, so sorry."

"Don't be. I asked you to do it."

I heard him grunt, then fall to the ground. I got no answer when I called out for him, asking what was going on. If I could only see him. If I could only get to him, ease his pain somehow.

But I couldn't.

I could only listen as he grunted in pain, as he slammed his fist against the marble floor. It sounded like he was biting back a scream, with only faint and desperate noises coming out. And just as quickly as it had begun, it stopped. He was quiet, eerily quiet.

"Castiel, what's going on?"

No answer. Suddenly, a deafening crash filled the room. I flung myself back as the bars from his cell shot forward, breaking from the wall. I frowned.

How did he do that?

I felt the color drain from my face when I got my answer. Castiel had his powers back.

No. The creature walking out of Castiel's cell had his powers back. He looked at me, and I gasped, backing up as far as I could. The black eyes were still there, and on his back sat a pair of massive black wings.

CHAPTER 21

Was it still him? I couldn't tell. Where he had looked somewhat human before now just looked... feral. But it *must* be Castiel. Somewhere under there, it must still be him. I inched forward slowly.

"Castiel? Do you know me?"

He tilted his head to the side, taking in my crouching form. "Of course."

Relief and dread mixed inside of me. "Do you feel like yourself?"

He shook his head. "No."

No. The fear trampled the small bit of relief I had felt to the ground. "Will you hurt me?" It pained me to ask, but how could I not?

He shook his head again. "No."

Well, that was always something, I suppose. Castiel stepped right up to the bars of my cell and gripped them tight. I covered my face when he pulled, the same ear-splitting sound as when he got out of his own cell.

I heard voices somewhere; there was probably going to be a whole swarm of angels down here soon. Castiel reached out his hand to me.

"Come."

I hesitated for a split second. It was still him, I told myself. He wasn't going to hurt me. So, I got to my feet and grabbed his outstretched hand. It was colder than normal, but still him.

Within seconds, the place filled with angels. They were all staring at Castiel, their raised swords falling at the sight of him. Gabriel pushed his way to the front, followed by some of the angels that had been sitting by the table earlier. I instantly recognized Michael. They looked almost as stunned at the sight of Castiel as the rest. Gabriel whirled his head around to me.

"What did you *do*?" He practically spat out the words.

"She didn't do this," Michael said. "Not entirely."

"What did?" I asked. I just needed to know.

"*They* did," Castiel answered in the archangel's

place. "When I fell, they stripped me of my soul. You just brought it back to life."

I wasn't sure if I believed that theory. Not entirely. The blackness I had felt inside him must be connected with this somehow. I must've triggered something when I tried to take away the darkness. Ironic, wasn't it? I tried taking it away, and it only amplified. My thoughts were interrupted by Gabriel's voice.

"She altered it somehow," he said. "Why else would you be so...?"

He didn't finish his sentence. Michael silenced him with one look. "Enough." He turned his attention back to us. His eyes were cold when he opened his mouth again. "Permission to kill the both of them. Right now."

My heart dropped to my stomach. The angels raised their swords again, but I could see the hesitation in their eyes. They were afraid of Castiel. With good reason, I would imagine. Castiel placed himself in front of me, his wings blocking off my view of the rest of them.

Then chaos broke out.

They charged at us, one after another. When they got close enough, Castiel started reaching for them with his bare hands. As he placed a hand to their heads, a terrible red light seemed to shine from within their skulls. Based on the way they slumped to the ground, their eyes turning dark like coal, I'd say he burned their insides.

My stomach flipped, and I tried to breathe calmly to keep myself from throwing up. The angels stopped in their tracks, but when Michael gave another order, they attacked again. More of the angels fell as Castiel put his hands on them, the air stinking with their burnt insides.

He couldn't get to them all, though. Castiel kept me behind his back, but there were too many. He couldn't keep track of both me and them. So, when I was jerked back, then pressed to the front of one familiar form, it was too late. I felt his blade before I saw it. Thinner than my own, and with a strange soft glow around the glassy steel. Gabriel was breathing heavily next to my ear.

"One move," he said. "One move, and I slice her throat."

Castiel stilled, and so did everybody else. "I will enjoy killing you," Castiel growled, pointing a finger right at Gabriel's face. "Let her go."

"I don't think so," Gabriel said, and the blade started cutting through my skin.

I felt a slight sting, and then a drop of blood ran down my throat. I could see the way Castiel tensed up, and I tried to press myself even closer to Gabriel to avoid the blade's edge. It didn't work.

"Enough of this!" Michael shouted, his voice booming across the silence. "End it, *now*."

It all seemed to happen at once. Swords being plunged into Castiels body as he rushed toward me, and the icy cold feel of the blade slicing across my throat.

The world fell away as my ears filled with Castiel's roar.

———

I COULD HEAR WATER. Birds. The rustle of leaves. But it all sounded so far away. Like I was listening to it under water. I didn't understand. Something felt off. I couldn't feel my magic, so I must still be in Heaven. But why did it smell like the forest?

I blinked my eyes open and gazed up at Castiel's blackened eyes. He pushed the hair out of my face, breathing out a sigh of relief.

"It worked," he said.

I tried to tell him that I didn't understand, but no sound came out. Whenever I tried to speak, a sharp pain shot through my throat. I reached a hand out to his, but my hand came away with dried blood. How was this possible? If Gabriel slit my throat, and I was lying there, alive... I really didn't get it.

"Don't try to speak," a familiar voice said somewhere off to the side. I turned my head, trying to ignore the head-splitting migraine I got as a result.

Tatia.

She sat a few feet away, her olive skin paler than usual. She looked like she was just about ready to pass out. Had she done this? Brought me back somehow? But that was impossible. Our magic didn't work like that. What was dead, stayed dead. There was no way around something as permanent as death.

I sat up, trying to ignore the way my head was spinning. I opened my mouth, but then I remembered that I couldn't speak.

"You will be able to speak again in a day or two," Tatia said. "Once your throat has a chance to heal."

"It might take longer than that with what's to come," Castiel said. Tatia nodded.

"I suppose."

I looked between the two, confusion written all over my face. Castiel put a hand to my cheek, making me focus in on him. "Gabriel killed you with his own blade."

"Heaven-kissed," Tatia filled in. I frowned. I had no idea what that meant.

Castiel seemed to understand my confusion. "When that blade was forged, a small part of Gabriel's soul was put into it. Every kill with such a blade would give the victim a kiss of Heaven. A fraction of the soul that lingered there."

"Castiel came to me with your body," Tatia explained. "Scared the sisters half to death. But that piece of Gabriel's soul was enough to weave together with your own. It was enough to bring you back."

Was she saying what I thought she was saying? If part of Gabriel's soul was mixed with my own, and I had died... I looked at Castiel, and he nodded, confirming my suspicion. Tatia came closer, placing a hand on my arm.

"Castiel tells me that it will be somewhat painful to

complete the transformation. But we are here to see you through it."

Fuck. Panic began to rise in my chest, and Castiel pulled me in close. "It's alright. I know you can handle it, Danika."

I wasn't a witch anymore. That's why I couldn't feel my magic. I had been altered by Gabriel's knife and Tatia's magic. I was going to become one of them.

An angel.

CHAPTER 22

They were right about one thing. The pain *was* excruciating. Despite screaming until I felt like I was going to pass out again, there was barely any noise coming out, thanks to my damaged vocal cords. It felt like someone was twisting my insides with tongs, or like I was being stabbed again and again. It seemed endless!

I saw glimpses of Castiel and Tatia every now and then, but it was like looking through frosted glass. I did see the rage on his face, though, and the fear in hers. I'm sure it was mirrored in my own.

When it felt like it was over, the worst had yet to come. The wings. Oh, no, the wings. I could *feel* them growing inside of me. Like a creature, trying to rip its way through flesh. This must be what Castiel had experienced back in the cell.

And when they finally did break through my back, I almost passed out. I *wish* I would've passed out. It was the most disgusting, foul feeling I had ever experienced. Castiel sat in front of me, although he didn't touch me as the white wings sprung forward from my back.

"It's almost over," he said.

I didn't believe him. It would never be over. It was all a lie. I hadn't survived when Gabriel slit my throat, after all, and this was my own personal Hell.

But it did end, of course. And it wasn't Hell; my feet were firmly placed on Earth. I was shaking, bile rising in my throat, but I could stand. Every cell in my body wasn't screaming in pain anymore. I still couldn't get a sound out, and I most likely wouldn't for a while with how I had been screaming. Damaging my already damaged vocal cords. But it was over. At least this part was done.

I saw Tatia first, her big eyes bigger still when she looked at me. "I can't believe this," she said quietly. "I can't believe this is you."

"Nor I."

I turned to the deep voice. Castiel came walking toward me, and I shuddered at the rage in those black eyes. He wiped away a tear that I hadn't even realized had been running down my cheek. I put my hand on top of his, keeping it on my face. I leaned into his touch, needing him to keep touching me. It was still him, I reminded myself for the thousandth time. Then a thought struck me.

Was I still me?

I felt like myself. And at the same time, not. The same was probably true for Castiel. There was such hatred on his face, though. I pulled him in and hugged him tightly. As long as there was no hatred for me, everything else could be worked through.

"Don't you worry," he whispered into my ear. "I will *end* him."

I nodded. I wanted Gabriel dead, too. But at the same time, what good would it do? Heaven was filled with more of his kind.

I pulled away and looked at Castiel. Placing a soft kiss on his lips, I shook my head.

Enough killing.

I hoped he understood. He looked displeased, so I assumed he did. *Good.*

"You should probably lay low for a while," Tatia said. "I'm afraid now they'll never stop chasing you."

"Let them come," Castiel huffed. "We'll end them all if they try."

I shook my head at him. This bloodthirst was apparently something I was going to have to get used to. I got out from under his arm and walked over to Tatia. There was so much I wanted to say to her. But since I couldn't, I simply took her hand in mine and pressed it to my lips. I tried to put every bit of love I had into that gesture and into the look I gave her. Her eyes were glassy, close to tears. I shook my head and caressed her cheek.

No tears.

"I'll miss you, Danika," she whispered quietly. "And so will the others. I hope we will meet again one day."

I nodded. I hoped so, too.

"We should get going," Castiel told me and put a hand to the small of my back. "Things are quiet. Too quiet. They'll be coming soon enough, and I want to put as much distance between us and them until then." He looked down at Tatia. "Will you be fine getting home?"

She nodded. "Don't worry about me. I'll manage. They have their eyes set on bigger fish than me."

"True enough," he said, and for the first time since becoming... whatever he was, there was a hint of a smile on his lips. "I wish you well, Tatia."

"Thank you. Look after her, okay?"

"I will." He turned his face to me again. "And I suspect she will look after me in return."

I smiled. No doubt about that.

We watched as Tatia walked away, back toward the city. I let myself take in the tall buildings and familiar sights. Maybe I'd be able to return someday. See the good parts of the place I'd grown up in, as well as the bad. I'd like that.

"Come," Castiel said and took my hand. "It's time to test out those wings of yours."

My stomach flipped at the thought. But with the nerves also came a hint of something else. Excitement. I had wings. I was going to *fly*.

"It's a bit tricky at first," he explained to me and spread his black wings wide. "But you have to trust yourself. It's in your nature to fly now."

I nodded, giving a silent gasp as I made my wings spread out. It was a strange feeling, and I was still a bit sore. But I found that I could move them with almost the same ease as an arm or a leg. They would take some getting used to, that's for sure.

"Crouch down slightly," Castiel instructed. "And when you push off, let your wings do the job. Are you ready?"

I swallowed hard, my palm sweaty in his grasp. Then I nodded.

We both crouched at the same time, and then Castiel counted down. On three, I pushed off from the ground, a thrill rising within me when I let the wings take over. I dropped a little at first, a silent scream escaping me. But I soon found a rhythm, and before I knew it, I was flying next to Castiel, higher and higher among the clouds.

It wasn't cold like it had been when Gabriel brought me to Heaven. It was just... incredibly freeing. Like swimming through the air. My face broke out into a giant grin.

"I'm never getting you back onto the ground now, am I?" Castiel asked, amusement on his face.

I shook my head, winking at him. No. Probably not.

We went as high up as we could while still keeping a safe distance from the barrier to Heaven. Castiel moved through the sky with such ease, and I tried to keep up.

I suppose I couldn't compare the two of us. He had been flying before I was even born. I'd get the hang of it eventually.

After an hour, we landed behind an old building, half torn to the ground. I needed to catch my breath, and we had to take more of those little breaks before we finally settled in for the night. I slept in his arms, his wings covering me like a dark, protective blanket.

I knew things would be difficult moving forward. I knew my old life was gone. I knew I would have to relearn how to be me. I also knew that Heaven was going to chase us down until the end of time. But in that moment, I only felt free. Because I was there with him.

And if we were going to be hunted down, why not cause some more trouble along the way?

An idea formed in my head before sleep finally took me.

EPILOGUE

My steps echoed between the buildings. My wings cast a shadow over the ground, my form lit up by the street lights that illuminated the night. I cast an eye at the sky, where I knew Castiel was flying somewhere. Waiting for my signal if I should need his help.

A weeping, hulking form laid on the ground a short bit ahead. Blood was gushing from his back where his wings had been. I rushed toward him, kneeling by his side, and placed a hand on his back. He flinched at the contact, but then he started to relax.

"You're not one of them, are you?" he asked, his voice cracking from all the crying. I shook my head.

"I'm here to help."

"They're not far from here," he said. "If they see you, you'll face the same punishment as me."

"Oh, don't worry about me," I said and carefully helped him into a sitting position. "I have backup, should they return."

He looked skyward. "Let's hope it's some damn good backup then."

"It is." I looked him in the eye. "What's your name?"

"Valerian."

"Well, Valerian," I said and placed his hand over his heart. "You have a choice to make. They have taken your wings and your powers. If you let me help you, then you can go on living your life down here on Earth. Or I can turn you into something else entirely."

"Into what, exactly?"

He had barely spoken the words before Castiel landed before us. I rose, taking in the stunning image of him. "Into something like that. You'll have your wings and your powers."

Valerian stared at the dark angel before him. "I've heard of you. The fallen with the blackened soul."

"Not fallen anymore," Castiel said. "But yes, that's me."

"They say you burn the insides of anyone you touch."

Castiel and I exchanged a look. His reputation was

certainly getting stronger. "Not quite. Not *everyone* I touch." Then he winked at me.

Valerian's eyes were wide, a mix of fear and awe when he looked at Castiel. "What's it like? Being like you?"

"It's not like before," Castiel explained. "But the brothers won't try to hurt you again if you choose this path. And if they do, that's the last thing they'll do."

Valerian swallowed. "I'm not sure."

"You have to decide," I told him. "If they return, then I won't be of much use."

He nodded. "Then I think I'd rather be human. But I have one more favor to ask of you."

"Name it."

He glanced at something behind me. No, not something. Someone. A young woman, clutching a small child to her chest, stepped out of the shadows. How had she managed to stay hidden from the angels? If they had seen her, she would've definitely been killed. I straightened.

"Your boy is Nephilim."

"Will you take that away from him?" he asked. "So we can live in peace?"

Micah's words from months ago ran through my head. I would take away what made the boy *him*. But when I saw the desperation on Valerian's face, I nodded. It was for the best. This way, they could all live a normal life together. I could give them that.

"Alright," I said. "Stand up. This might hurt."

Valerian laughed. "Can't imagine it hurting more than having my wings torn off my back."

I suppose he was right. I placed my hand over his and put them over his heart. I may not have had my old powers, but I had new ones. Angelic ones. The process was still similar as back when I used to strip Nephilim of their powers. Just faster and less draining.

I found the blackened piece that was the fallen angel's soul. Cleansed it from the tainted powers the others had left there. Severed all ties with the angelic parts of him. He groaned but remained standing.

It was done within minutes. The process was equally simple with the boy. He cried a little, but only for a short while. The relief on the mother's face was palpable.

"Is it over?" she asked. "They won't come for them anymore?"

"No," I said. "They won't."

The young woman turned to Valerian, and there was so much love in the look they shared that I had to turn away. It was *their* moment.

Instead of the family, I looked at my own love, Castiel. My family. I still missed my sisters, but I knew they were alright with Tatia at the helm. I had no place amongst them anymore.

The family thanked us again, and Castiel took my hand when we left them. He kissed my knuckles, then looked up. "They're close."

"They didn't get to them in time," I said. "Valerian and the boy." Sure, he had lost his wings, but he could now live out his life with his loved ones. Heaven didn't win.

"No." Castiel smiled. "They won't get to any of them, thanks to you."

I hoped that would one day be true. That my meddling would end the way Heaven treated the fallen and their Nephilim children. Until then, I was there. Helping them every step of the way.

We stopped, and Castiel leaned in and kissed me softly. I smiled into the kiss, loving that despite the anger that lived inside him, he still kissed me with such tenderness. With such love.

"On to the next place?" he asked when we broke apart. I nodded.

We crouched down and pushed off the ground, letting our wings carry us to a new place. I held onto him, found my strength in Castiel's touch. We would always be hunted. Always. But they would never win. Not with their dwindling numbers and their own people turning on them and their laws. There were more people like Valerian out there.

And I would always get to them all before Heaven did.

Always.

ABOUT THE AUTHOR

Viola Tempest is a dystopian fantasy and paranormal romance author who yearns to expose the truth of those in the modern world: the good, the bad, and the ugly. Her inspiration primarily stems from life experiences, those who annoy her, ex-boyfriends, and the crazy dreams that pop into her head every once in a while.

STALK HER BELOW!

Website:
https://www.violatempest.com/

Facebook Page:
https://www.facebook.com/authorviolatempest

Instagram:
https://www.instagram.com/author_violatempest/

Goodreads:
https://www.goodreads.com/author/show/
21693342.Viola_Tempest

Bookbub:
https://www.bookbub.com/authors/viola-tempest

saving
the
fallen

VIOLA TEMPEST

www.ingramcontent.com/pod-product-compliance
Lightning Source LLC
Chambersburg PA
CBHW031231210726
48287CB00003B/748